SUPERN
Dating Agency

Phwoar
and
Peace

ANDIE M. LONG

Happy reading

This book is dedicated to Withernsea.

Andie M. Leg

PROLOGUE

Since they had vanquished me, I'd been in a state of nothingness. I existed, but I didn't. Like being in a black room, with no sounds, and spending 99.9% of time asleep.

Then something had changed. Like the spark of a pilot light, a tiny glow filled the black space. I didn't know how, but I could detect I was nothing but a tiny collection of dark matter. Thoughts and images began to fill the void.

I saw a vision of Shelley bloody Landry. She was under the sea by the looks of it. I saw a bride run off with, was that Simon Cowell? And then I saw Shelley tell her sister to 'Go get your man'.

Ha!

She had made a binding deal with me that she

wouldn't match-make anyone supernatural and here she had just broken it. For Drake was a supe and at her words Polly and Drake moved towards each other, kissed, and got together.

Ha!

But now what? I was back, but not much use in this state. They had filled my previous position as Satan after they had vanquished me, so what did I do next?

More images came into view as the dark matter I was developed sight. I was in Beached, the restaurant where I had been vanquished. It made sense I would return to the same spot.

I felt myself called toward the farmhouse. Images and information swept into me, causing my ball of energy to enlarge slightly.

As I hovered outside of the farmhouse window, I saw the small top window was open and I swept inside. Oh dear. Looked like any wards Shelley had put up to keep the family safe didn't work against a ball of something unidentifiable. What a shame! Moving into the living room, images swept into me of the werewolf giving birth. Wow, it was the woman I'd tried to incinerate from the inside out. She'd given birth to werebabies no less. I assessed the newborns. Too young. I couldn't take over them.

But I learned of a husband who remained in fear of supernatural beings, and what was that? He had a fear of being possessed? Oh how ironic.

I plucked the address of Mark Linley from his wife's mind and moved on to an address in Hull.

It was so kind of Mark to also have left a window open. Once I took over his body, I realised it was one of his wife's pet hates. Always opening windows, even when it was freezing cold outside. I needed to practice walking in this middle-aged body. My last one, the vampire Reuben's, had been a lot more aesthetically pleasing. I vowed to join a gym first thing in the morning. This getting Withernsea back under my rule was not to be rushed; my evil plans would have to stay on the down low until the time was right to make my move. I couldn't take Withernsea back if I couldn't run to the bus stop without collapsing.

I walked over to the window and closed it firmly. Wouldn't want to annoy my little wifey. It had been a while since I'd got some. Mrs Debbie Linley was in for a devil of a time and one hell of a ride with her new hot husband...

CHAPTER 1

SHELLEY

"Theo, I don't know about getting the bed-and-breakfast open soon, with the amount of people we have here, I think you are already up and running, albeit not being paid."

After the events of the day, I could have done with a hot bath and an early night with a good book, and yes, I said book. However, I had come home to find my best friend on my best sofa where she promptly soaked it in amniotic fluid before birthing her triplet cubs. She never did do things by halves. Right now, I had the new mom, daughter, two sons, and a brand-new over-protective alpha werewolf father in my living room; my adoptive mother, and my daughter in the kitchen; and my sister and her boyfriend had disappeared upstairs, most likely to do things I didn't want to visualise.

"Yes, indeed. I think this week I will finalise all my plans for the bed-and-breakfast to get it open as soon as possible. That way the rooms will hopefully be full to capacity and will therefore prevent half of our family and friends in Withernsea from turning up here every five seconds."

"If it's okay with you, Theo, I will go to your office to order a new sofa. Once Kim and Darius finally leave, if you could use that special vampire speed to whizz my now ruined sofa off to the tip, I'll steam the carpet."

I wasn't sure I'd ever be able to sit in my living room again without the harrowing image of my best friend's vagina hurtling into my mind. I'd come to expect the unexpected with Kim, but on this occasion she had surpassed herself. It was only the fact that I now had three new babies I could cuddle that meant I'd forgive her for ruining my best sofa. With Charlene's rapid growth I'd not been able to enjoy much of the baby stage, so with any luck if I could get past the new father I'd be able to have lots of baby cuddles.

The kitchen door opened and my adoptive mum walked through into the hallway. "I'm going to make my way home now, Shelley, as your dad has just called to tell me he's cooked dinner. I should've threatened him with divorce fifteen years ago. He said again how he wants to get to know all of you better but given he has only recently threatened to out all supernaturals, he understands it will take you a while to trust him. In the meantime, he's leaving it for me to pave the way."

She wasn't kidding. It was going to take more than one message through my mother to believe Mark Linley had suddenly changed his ways. Right now, I had other priorities.

As she stood in the doorway, Debbie turned back to me, "Say goodbye to Polly for me. It was a shame her headache came on like that. I hope Drake is looking after her properly. Anyway, I'll be off. After tea, I have all my selfies with Simon Cowell to show the neighbours."

Thank God the photos would just appear to have been taken in an elaborate building and that the water didn't show on photos. Closing the door behind her, I let out a large sigh. I decided I needed a large cup of Jax's coffee before I did anything else. Even ordering the new sofa would have to wait while I sat at my kitchen table and took five. Charlie was already sitting there. She took one look at my face, jumped up, and switched the kettle on while getting the coffee and a mug out of the cupboard.

"It was a bit selfish of Auntie Polly to disappear

upstairs with Drake. It's not like any of us believed she truly had a headache. We all know she's gone upstairs to shag his brains out."

"Charlie! Watch your language."

"Oh come on, Mum. You need to have a word with her. It's not fair leaving us to have to put up with Debbie." She finished making me a coffee and placed it in front of me at the table. "I'm going up to my room now. It's been a long day, and I need to ring Alyssa to see what's going down with her and the barista."

There was a roar from the living room. The door rattled on its hinges and an angry alpha male thundered into the kitchen.

"Charlie, what's this about someone going down on my sister?" He looked ready to rip off heads.

"Darius, that's not what she said. Charlie is going to ring Alyssa to see what's going down with her and Bartholomew, the barista." I was going to get a headache if I rolled my eyes any more today.

A tumultuous growl rattled the kitchen windows.

"Mum, I don't think that's helping." She looked at Darius. "Don't worry, nothing is going on between them. Alyssa just has a girl crush, like a teen thing. Anyway, once she knows she has a new niece and two nephews, she should be far too busy for boys."

With this, Darius visibly relaxed. His shoulders

dropped away from his ears and he let out a large exhale. "Sorry, some kind of biological protection mode seems to have set in, making me some kind of supercharged alpha. I apologise if I have broken even more furniture or doors."

"I'll get you a coffee, Darius," Charlie said.

"Forget that," Theo told her, coming into the kitchen. "Darius, let me get you a beer to celebrate and wet the babies' heads."

"So I push three babies out of my hooha and he gets alcohol? Get back in here, Darius Wild, this instant." Kim's voice echoed off the walls.

"Looks like I'm going to have to wait. Raincheck, though?"

"Sure," Theo replied.

"Yeah, raincheck until the kids have left home, mate. No way are you leaving me at home with three screaming children while you go out on the piss. That's my job," Kim hollered through the open door of the living room. "Now, when you've all finished, do you think someone could bring *me* a coffee? Also, Shelley, I know your clothes are on the large size for me, but do you have something I could wear, only I'm sitting here in a damp dress with a towel between my legs."

She'd get 'clothes on the large size'. For that she

could wear my unicorn onesie, the cow. The supposed horn on its head looked like a penis gone wrong. That was the problem with random internet purchases. Things didn't always look the same as on the photos when they arrived.

I excused Charlie from making the drinks and let her escape to her room. Darius went back in to Kim, taking his mobile phone from his pocket ready to ring his family to tell them about the new arrivals. He assured me that shortly he, Kim, and the babies would be on their way back home and that we wouldn't be getting the entire Withernsea pack arriving at the door at any moment.

I closed my eyes for a time while I sat in the kitchen. I inhaled the wonderful aroma of the coffee and tasted a delicious mouthful.

"Are you bringing me some clothes or leaving me to freeze to death? You just enjoy a drink after your hard day schmoozing with Mr Cowell. It's not like I want to get in my own bed or anything."

For the love of God. I'd spent the day smoothing out the politics of the sea and dealing with a hysterical sister, and now I was dealing with my belligerent bestie. All I'd wanted was one damn coffee in peace. I ran upstairs and got the onesie out and brought it down. I burst into the living room, and once I could see she wasn't holding any of the newborns, I threw it at her. "There are some pants, a few sanitary pads you are lucky I found because I don't have any of that any more being undead, and this nice cosy onesie."

She gave me a look that would have killed the Grim Reaper himself.

"I hope you get a hearty satisfaction from watching your best friend, who is exhausted from birthing three babies, dress in this heinous outfit. This is how the pack will greet me when I get home." She dressed in it and pulled up the hood. I could see Darius was struggling to keep a straight face. "It is actually extremely comfortable." She tipped her chin at me. "I may adopt onesies as my new daily attire."

"Or you could just stay as a wolf with all your fur..." Darius looked at her perplexed.

"I'd rather not. I've spent the best part of my life shaving and waxing hair off and then suddenly I'm supposed to deal with it being everywhere. I'll stick mainly to my human form and these terribly crass but amazingly comfortable all-in-ones. And look, it has a zipper all the way down the front for easy access to the milking station for the cubs."

She picked up one of the babies. "Come on, Beiber. Let's get you, Taylor, and Bublé home."

She looked at our dropped mouths. "God, you're all just suckers. As if I'd call my children that."

Shit. I'd lost the sweepstakes we'd held in the coffee shop. Just for a moment there, the prize had been within reach.

CHAPTER 2

CHARLIE

I was glad to get to my room after the busy events of the day. Though I needed to call my best friend, I knew Darius was about to ring her about her new niece and nephews. I decided I'd shoot her a quick text and ask her to call me when she was free.

But when I laid on my bed and took my phone from my bag to ring her, the only shooting in my life was a pain once again going down my legs. This had been happening since the latter part of the non-wedding. I'd not mentioned it to anyone as there was enough going on.

Pain like I'd never known coursed through me, so bad that my body couldn't take it, and everything went black.

I woke to darkness. Staring at the clock, I saw over three hours had passed. I reached over to switch on my bedside light. When had I fallen asleep? It was then I remembered the pain I'd experienced. I'd better go tell my mum about it. She'd know what to do. Maybe I'd picked up a virus? I shuffled my feet into my slippers. Stupid things, what was wrong with them? They felt a size too small. I kicked them away in disgust and opened my bedroom door.

My father was right outside, making his way downstairs.

He turned quickly around and screamed.

That made me scream.

He screamed again.

"Dad. Stop it. For goodness' sake. It's been enough of a dramatic day already. You're not treading the boards now, you know?"

He peered at me, coming closer.

"Ch-Ch-Charlie?"

"D-D-Dad?" I deadpanned. What the heck was wrong with him? Parents were so weird.

Mum came to the bottom of the stairs.

"What on earth is all the screaming about? Haven't

we had enough dramatics for one day? I'm trying to enjoy just a bit of peace and quiet."

My dad beckoned for her to come upstairs. Sighing, and moaning about never getting a minute, she stomped up every step. Then she took one look at me and screamed.

"Not you too. What is it? Do I have a massive zit on my nose or something? Has a spider crawled on my head in the night?"

I strolled over to the large wall mirror and stopped in my tracks.

Because Charlene Landry, the teenager, was no more. Charlene Landry, the woman, looking around her early twenties, stared back at me from the mirror. My hair was a good six inches longer, reaching below my more than ample breasts. I was about four inches taller. No doubt I'd gone up a size or two in shoes, hence my slippers not fitting. It was a good job I'd worn a loose tunic style dress to the wedding that had finished below the knee as now my dress skimmed halfway down my thighs. Another inch or two and it would have been indecent.

"That's why I passed out," I declared.

"You did what?" My mum came rushing over to me. "Come on, let's get you checked over."

"She doesn't leave this house tonight," my father said in a stern voice.

"Well, that's a bit overcautious, Theo. If she seems okay, I'm sure she'll be all right."

"She. Doesn't. Leave. This. House. *EVER!*"

My mum narrowed her eyes at him. "What on earth has got into you, Theo? Go get some O-neg and calm yourself down. She passed out and she'll be okay. It was no doubt growing pains while she became an adult."

"An adult." My dad started pacing. "An adult. An adult who can have sex, Shelley. Do you understand what I'm saying?"

The penny dropped with my mum.

"Ah."

"I'm not going out tonight, Dad," I reassured him. "This change has wiped me out. Once Mum checks me over, I'm going to eat, drink, and sleep."

"Fabulous." He beamed.

"Then I'll be fully recovered for tomorrow," I said winking at him.

"Shelley!"

My mother put a silence spell on him. Dad didn't know and kept gasping, looking like a fish out of water.

"I know you're thinking about meeting Kai," my

mum said. But we need to make sure you're okay after this new change. Anyway, let's get you checked over. I'll pop us both over to the caves and we can see the medics there. Hold tight."

But before she could whizz us there, Mum's phone rang. She plucked it from her pocket, pressed answer and held it to her ear.

"Shelley!" I could hear Ebony's voice from here. "I'm on my way home. The war, it's started. I keep seeing fire. Lots and lots of fire, and... sausage rolls."

"Anything else? Like who's behind it? No? Okay, Ebs. We'll assemble a meeting for tomorrow around half eleven at the coffee shop. Give you time to get back. In the meantime, we'll be extra vigilant."

"Have there been any strange happenings at your end?"

"Other than weretriplets being born and arguments under the sea? No." Mum shook her head even though Ebony couldn't see her. Then she looked at me and her eyes widened.

"Oh, actually, there might have been something..."

She put the phone away and looked at me. "So, if you didn't hear her shrieking down the phone, Ebony believes the war is starting. It's possible that this is why you've grown to adulthood. Let's get you checked over straightaway." She removed the silence spell from Dad and whizzed us straight out of there.

Dominica met us at the caves and gave me a full physical exam and checked my bloods etc. "There's nothing untoward. You've just had a growth spurt," she reassured me.

"We think it might signal the start of the great war, so please advise everyone here to be on the alert." Mum told her.

"We will. Although we're always on the alert here anyway." The caves were a place where enemies were held captive as well as a place for healing. "If you need us to rally, just say the word, Charlie."

It was strange being spoken to with such reverence, and the focus not being on Mum but on me. It seemed the time had come for me to take my rightful place as the Queen of Withernsea.

I yawned heartily. I could only pray I was up to the job, but right now I needed sleep like a vampire needed blood. As my mum whizzed me back home, I must have fallen asleep in her arms, as the next thing I knew it was morning and I was back in my own bed. I stared at the Shawn Mendes posters on my wall, and looked around at all the other teenage paraphernalia, including clothes that were now too small for me strewn all over the bedroom furniture and the floor. Before queenly duties commenced, I figured I needed to do a touch of clearing up.

CHAPTER 3

SHELLEY

L ate Saturday morning, it was all hands on deck at the coffee shop as the place was packed to the brim with the residents of Withernsea. There was myself, Theo, and Charlie; My mum Margret and my father Dylan; Frankie and Lucy; Ebony and Henry; Samara and her husband Johnny; Jax and Tristan; Polly and Drake; Duke Brishon; Rav; the new queen of the fairies, Ella; and one or two other supernaturals. Kai wasn't here. Charlie told me that she'd asked him to stay away for his own safety. Debbie was here too. I knew she was trying to make an effort, but I could have done without having to explain everything to her every five seconds, especially about the fact her 'grandaughter' had grown again.

We were just waiting for the new mum now,

although I'd called and told her I would understand if she didn't show today. I figured she'd be exhausted after no doubt being up most of the night with the babies. But this was my best friend, and she was determined not to miss out on a thing.

The door crashed open and what I think was my best friend half fell through it, staggering over to the nearest chair which happened to have Samara in it. She dragged Samara out of it using her wolf strength and when Samara began to protest, my bestie full on growled at her, making all heads that weren't already turned in her direction swivel around in shock. She then dropped down on the chair, resting her arms on the table in front of her. Her head promptly fell forward atop her arms and there she stayed.

Behind her followed Darius, with one baby in a papoose snuggled into his front. Alyssa followed, in full auntie duty, pushing a double buggy containing two more babies. Thankfully, all three babies seemed to be asleep... like their mother.

Darius took one look at Kim and turning his gaze on me, shrugged his shoulders. "I told her to stay at home. She wouldn't listen."

Everyone began cooing around the babies. Darius had his daughter in the papoose. She had almost died during her birth and had been saved by Polly with a healing power which had probably now transferred to the baby. Only time would tell, but the power was no longer with Polly.

"What have you decided to call them?" Lucy asked Darius. "They're Kim's, so I went for Chardonnay, Merlot, and Zinfandel."

Frankie elbowed her muttering, "They don't know about the sweepstakes."

"My daughter is called Louisa, which means 'strong and valiant fighter'. My sons are Cedric, which means 'warrior leader' as he was born first; and Finian, which means 'handsome warrior'. Finian is the baby with the mole on his right cheek."

I swear every woman in the coffee shop swooned at Darius' announcement and the sweepstakes were instantly forgotten. My best friend's hunky husband had stood tall and proud as he introduced his first cubs, and we'd all got a good view of arm-porn as he flexed his muscles indicating each newborn in turn.

"Gorgeous names for gorgeous babies," I told him. "Take a seat and I'll get you a coffee. I'll get your wife about four." I turned to ask Alyssa if she wanted a drink, but she already held one in her hand, no doubt courtesy of Bartholomew, the barista she'd been out on a date with. I made sure Darius' chair faced in the opposite direction, so he didn't tear Bartholomew limb from limb.

When everyone had refreshments, I called for their attention. Everyone fell silent.

"Thank you all for attending today at such short notice, especially given how busy we've all been lately. We are led to believe by certain events that war may indeed be coming to Withernsea imminently. Therefore, we all need to be extremely vigilant about any changes around us, any signs of evil etc. Firstly, we're going to hear from Ebony, our seer, about her visions. Over to you, Ebs."

Ebony rose and cleared her throat. It was at that point we all heard a large miaow at the door.

I moved my gaze to see a black cat scratching at the door trying to get in.

Kim raised her head, looked at the doorway and shouted, "Someone shoo that bloody thing away." She then noticed the coffee in front of her and drank three down one after the other.

Lucy got up and opened the door, letting the cat in. It dashed to the back of the room.

"What are you doing? Ah!" Kim said as her eyes finally appeared to register the daylight and her brain woke up. "Maisie."

The next minute, the sexiest woman in Withernsea, AKA Maisie the werecat, swaggered over to the table and sat down. Seriously, we all would. There was a reason she'd been crowned Miss Werecat 2015. She had long dark hair, chocolate skin, deep dark eyes that held you in their depths, chiselled cheekbones, pouty lips, and an hourglass figure. But mess with Maisie and you knew about it. This kitten definitely had claws. Bartholomew's tongue was hanging out and Alyssa's jaw set tight before she stomped over to the tables to sit next to Charlie.

"As you were," Maisie said. "Sorry, I was late. There was something fishy outside."

"There you go, wife. Ask her what she saw," Theo said. "My wife has just asked about any unusual activity in the area."

"I meant someone had left half of their cod in the bins near the chip shop," Maisie told him.

"Oh." Theo shut up.

I clapped my hands together. "Okay, as we were, people. Ebony, over to you. Please tell everyone about your vision."

Ebony swallowed and took a deep breath. "I see fire, and I feel strong heat, like I am burning up. It comes with an overwhelming feeling of terror inside me." Ebony clutched at her throat dramatically.

"Sure, you're not just trying to cook dinner again?" Kim quipped.

I threw her a warning glare. "Is that all the information so far?" I double checked with Ebony.

"Well... I see... I see... sausage rolls."

"Where?" Kim's eyes shot towards the counter, and she sat up extra straight. Her eyes were wide—the caffeine had kicked in. "I'm starving. Grab me three, Jax. One for each of the babies I've birthed."

Jax shook her head. "We don't have sausage rolls today. Just doughnuts."

"Oh, I'll have three of those then. Thanks, lovely."

Lucy scratched her head, looking around. "Where are you seeing sausage rolls, Ebony?"

Ebony's face took on a grey pallor. It always freaked the living daylights out of me. She looked like the 'bent neck lady' from *The House on Haunted Hill*, albeit with her neck intact—for now—because I had a feeling if she shouted out about any more foodstuffs not available in the cafe, Kim would wring it.

"The heat is intense."

"Does it come with a smell?" I asked her. "Burning?"

"Just so very hot." Ebony began opening her blouse, revealing a black lacy bra with nipple cut-outs. Looked

28

like the honeymoon period was alive and well. Henry dived at her, pulling her blouse back together. "Can't breathe. It's so hot." Then as fast as she said that, she stood still. "Sausage rolls. A plate of sausage rolls. War. It's war."

The colour returned to her face and Ebony opened her eyes. She looked down to see her new husband holding her blouse together.

"For heaven's sake, Henry. At least wait until we get home." She shook him off her and refastened her blouse, sitting down.

"Okay, thank you, Ebony. Moving swiftly on, Frankie will now talk to us about what he has unearthed about the prophecy during his in-depth research over the last few months. You will remember that Frankie holds a database about all the supernaturals of Withernsea which is of great use to us all."

Frankie stood up. He looked like shit, with his hair all over the place and dark circles under his eyes. He and Theo should have been in bed now. Being up in the daylight hours went completely against their vampire body clocks and could make them feel quite poorly. But his help was needed today, so he'd stayed up.

Frankie looked down at the small piece of paper in his hand. I'd been expecting him to be carrying a large folder. He'd obviously condensed his research down for us all. How thoughtful.

"My research discovered the following: that a female child would be born, and she would be the descendant of different supernatural creatures. Each generation would develop new powers through the pairing of different species. The father would be a vampire and her mother descended from wyverns. The child would be the strongest Withernsea had ever seen, would rule Withernsea and Wyvern Sea, and she would save us from war."

"And what about this war? What information do we have about that?" I asked him. "Who starts it? Supe or human? When does it begin?"

Frankie looked at me blankly. "That's it. That's all there is."

I scrubbed a hand through my hair. "So, basically what we already know from Ebony's visions?"

Frankie nodded enthusiastically. "That is correct."

I had a pain in my eye and rubbed it. These people were taking years off my life. Then I remembered I was an undead vampire. It still took some getting used to.

"So Charlie's going to save us from a great war involving heat and sausage rolls? Better get yourself down to Gregg's, Chaz, for when the last one comes out of the oven." Kim rolled her eyes.

"Kim!" Darius admonished.

"Well, I got dressed for this! I could have stayed inside in my lovely warm house, sitting on my pile ring in my onesie while the triplets took it in turns to drink me dry. But instead, I come here, where only Shelley is looking after me because I still haven't been given any doughnuts." She glared at Jax who scurried to put some on a plate.

Darius stood up and in his deep growly voice he apologised for his wife's behaviour. "If you could please wrap up some doughnuts for me to take away, Jax. I am sorry, my wife is suffering from sleep deprivation which is affecting her moods."

"Really? I couldn't tell the difference from her usual demeanour," Lucy quipped.

"Your turn will come, bitch. See if you're so funny when your vagina is on fire."

"Sweetie, I used to do that for fun down in hell. Fire play. Don't knock it until you've tried it." Lucy winked. "Actually everyone, don't try it. There are special flames and protection in hell. Here you'd melt your genitals off and need the hospital."

I needed to call this meeting back to order. How we'd got from the war in Withernsea to a conversation about genitals so fast was beyond me.

"Is there anything else before we call this meeting to a close?"

"Yes," Duke Brishon stood up. "We need to perform the ceremony for Princess Charlene post-haste. She needs to become queen now she is an adult. Therefore, we need to de-crown you and coronate her. Can you make it Monday evening, say eight pm?"

"Yes. Thank you, Duke Brishon. Indeed, the quicker Charlene is made queen, the better." That was mainly because then they'd stop throwing dirty seawater at me.

We closed the meeting, and everyone made their way out, including Polly and Drake who had gathered their belongings and were moving into his house under the water. Finally, we seemed to be getting our home back to ourselves.

I remained in the coffee shop with Charlie. I wanted to have a chat with my daughter about the future.

"Off you go to bed, Theo. I'll see you tonight," I told him. "And straight to bed. No more looking up waterproof chastity belts."

A certain vampire was still struggling to process the fact his daughter was growing up fast. Well, I guess she had only been born in February...

CHAPTER 4

CHARLIE

O h God. Now my mother wanted to have a
word with me. I hope it didn't involve a sex
talk. How embarrassing was this going to be? My
schedule was already a bit full on. Let me see. I
counted on my fingers.

1. Get used to being in my twenties.
2. Reassure Alyssa that we were still friends, seeing as I
was now a lot older than her.
3. Chat to Alyssa about Bartholomew—who was also a
lot older than her.
4. Become queen of Wyvern Sea.
5. Look out for impending war with special attention
to any fire, heat, and sausage rolls!!!!

6. Try to get past my dad to see Kai, my hunky merman.

7. Throw off the last traces of being fifteen which kept tripping my system, ie wanting to stomp about in protest at my dad's behaviour and call him lame.

But one thing at a time and first it was catch up time with my mum, who I had to say was really looking in need of a coffee right now.

"What are you counting? Is it days to the war? Do you know something?" she panicked; her face creased in concern.

"Nope, just how many things are on my 'to-do' list. I'll get us both a fresh coffee, Mum. Take five."

Alyssa was hanging around the counter throwing shade at Maisie who hadn't left yet. I watched as Maisie stalked up to the front of the shop. She stood next to Alyssa and leaned in.

I dashed over ready to protect my friend, if need be, only to hear Maisie say, "Baby girl, I don't want your man. He's a weak human. Anyway, out of the two of you, you're far more attractive. Shame I'm a cat, and you're a dog. Not a good mix." She wrinkled her nose.

Alyssa's face contorted. "I am not a dog. I am a wolf."

Maisie laughed and headed to the door. "You lot are so easy to wind up. You need to not give a shit. Be more cat. Ciao, miaow." With that she left.

I ordered my drinks from Bartholomew.

"Are you around later?" I asked my best friend.

Alyssa's lips drooped. "Look at you, Charlie. You're gorgeous; all grown up and the queen-to-be. Let's face it, you don't need me anymore."

Sighing, I rolled my eyes at her. "That's not true, but right now I have to chat with my mother. We need a catch up later. By the way, you're being too clingy around Sir Loins. It's true that sometimes you have to treat them mean to keep them keen."

She quirked a brow. "Are you going to be mean to Kai when you see him?"

My heart stuttered for a moment and my stomach flipped. "Shit, I can't even think about that right now. I'm so nervous. Anyway, talk later. Get out of here, Lys." I took my phone out of my pocket and sent her a text.

Alyssa took hers out of her pocket and read it.

Charlie: Pretend you got a text from a guy from the pack.

"Oh, Dermot back at Wiv, wants to see me about some pack stuff. That'll be a hardship given he's fucking hot."

I elbowed her. "Ooooh, try to take a pic."

Bartholomew came over to the counter with my drinks. "Dermot, you say? Oh, I was just going to see if you wanted to hang around the coffee shop with me, Alyssa. It's almost my lunch break." His high-pitched voice grated on me, but Alyssa was obviously immune, or prepared to tolerate it for his hot body.

Alyssa looked at me. I texted her again.

Charlie: It's working. Go!!!

Alyssa shrugged her shoulders. "Another time maybe, hun. Although it's a bit lame me hanging around here anyway." She turned to me. "Bye, babes. I'll let you know if I'm free later, or if Dermot's keeping me busy." She gave me a wink and left the coffee shop looking a lot happier than before.

I smiled at Bartholomew, who struggled to smile back. Then I thanked him for the drinks and headed back towards my mum.

"Thanks, love. I'm most definitely ready for this drink after this morning. It was all rather a waste of time in the end. We're no further forward, are we?"

"I guess not, but you know, Mum, if there's one thing my super-speedy aging has taught me, it's that life is for living. I have no real idea of how long I'm going to be around. I have a feeling that my vamp genes will kick in and I'll stay this kind of age for a while, but what if I don't? What if in a week's time, I'm like a hundred?"

My mum bit her lip. "Aww, Mum, don't get sad. I know this must be weird, but I'm a prophecy, here to save Withernsea. Maybe that's my entire purpose?"

My mum shook her head. "I can't believe that, Charlie. I *won't* believe that."

She leaned back in her seat and let out a huge sigh. "Do you know what? It's not even a year yet since I met your father. This time last year, I thought I was human. When I think about everything that has happened from then until now my mind is blown. I hope the war really is some nonsense about the last sausage roll in Greggs so that we can just get on with our lives and relax for a little while. Maybe I could spend some time shopping with my beautiful daughter rather than having to discuss saving the world."

"Shopping! Mum, that's what I need to do. Go to Ebony's next. Only I've grown out of all my clothes."

My mum laughed, which was nice to see because she hadn't had much cause to do so lately. "I know they say kids grow out of stuff overnight, but I think you're taking things a step too far."

I chuckled along with her.

"If you weren't such a short arse, I could borrow your stuff."

"Is it my fault you're five foot ten? You can blame your dad for that one!"

"My mum is only a few years older than me, and my father is 127. And you think I'm weird."

"Talking about your dad..."

"Oh, Mum. I'm not going to avoid or delay seeing Kai just to appease my dad. I've already said life is for living. Kai was my future, and he's now my present. He's my one."

"I know, darling. That's not what I was going to say. I was going to say you need to see Kai when your dad's asleep or tell him you're meeting Alyssa. You just have to be clever and remember your dad is highly intelligent, has super-strength hearing, speed, and has come across a hell of a lot of lies in 127 years, so you'll need to get creative. And of course I can't be seen to be helping you meet your boyfriend. So, I've said my bit, just... be gentle around your father. He's a sensitive man. Also, he killed his own family so he probably wouldn't think twice about draining Kai."

"Duly noted." I took a nice big drink of my coffee.

"I got the rest of your results back from Dominica at the caves this morning, and it would appear that you are indeed now part vampire, part witch, and also are coming up as having traces of pixie, faerie, and shifter. It has come along the birth-line and all mixed to become you. Tonight, after tea, I want to transfer the wyvern part over to you, Charlie. It's time."

"But, Mum. You've only held that power for such a short space of time from Grandad passing it onto you."

"Its home is within you, Charlie, and I believe that's where it will stay. That your own children, should you have them, will be a beautiful mix of you and your husband, but that the Force majeure will always be you. I think your vampire aging will kick in. I don't think you're destined to go anywhere or look geriatric any time soon."

Mum finished her drink and nodded towards the door. "Right, shall we get you some new clothes? Particularly ones that will appeal to a certain merman?"

I quickly swallowed the last of my own drink down.

"Oooh. What's my budget, Mum, for a new wardrobe? You know with Dad's millions in the bank."

"Ssh." Mum looked around in a panic. "No one

must ever know. A vampire's wealth can bring a lot of enemies. It's not their fault they've worked and banked for so many years. But," she whispered. "Let's have a spree. We'll start next door and then there's Tesco's and the couple of shops on Queen's Street."

Some of my Facebook friends talked about shopping malls and centres. We had Ebony's, two shops that were converted terraced houses, and a small bit of Tesco's. Oh well. We also had the power to magic a glamour over ourselves of every outfit in the world so there was that. I think maybe I might just glamour the Victoria's Secret Dream Angels VS Fantasy bra on myself especially for Kai. The £767k one designed by Atelier Swarovski. At least there were some perks to being the saver of Withernsea.

As we entered Ebony's boutique there didn't seem to be anyone around. Then we heard shuffling from behind the counter and a ruffled-haired seer stood up. "Good morning. How—"

"Ebony Marston. What are you up to down there?" My mum's eyes widened.

Henry stood up, smoothing down his shirt. "Well,

I'd better get off to work. Those walls won't paint themselves." He slunk out of the doorway past our amused faces.

"Henry was just helping me because I'd dropped—"

"Unless the answer is your panties, Ebs. Save it. Because none of us here are stupid," Mum told her.

Ebony pulled a mirror in front of her and quickly brushed her hair. "That's better," she said in her cut-glass accent. "Would you like to borrow it, Shelley?" She held out her brush.

"No, I'll stay my dishevelled self, thank you, *friend*. Today, it's all about getting Charlie kitted out in a whole new wardrobe. She needs everything, Ebs. Undies, clothes, shoes, more grown-up accessories."

"I have a new range of ladies vibrators. They are a very sophisticated design. It's a new product line I was hoping to introduce before the wedding, only I didn't have time. They're in the back. Excuse me a moment while I go fetch them."

"I meant bracelets and earrings, Ebony. I've not come to buy my daughter a sex toy."

"Right, indeed." Ebony smiled a 'customer is always right smile', ie it was more of a grimace. "Well, Charlie. Thank you for looking after the store for me while I was on my honeymoon. You did a truly fabulous job, so all it takes for me to say now is, you're fired."

I looked at her, my mouth dropped open.

"What?"

CHAPTER 5

CHARLIE

I'd done a great job so now I was fired? How did that work?

"Ebs, that doesn't seem justified. I was hoping I'd get a pay rise not the sack," I grumbled.

She shrugged her shoulders. "I'm sorry, darling, but you now need to focus your energies on saving Withernsea and so having to come here on a daily basis cannot happen. You'd be too distracted by the new stock and might miss a clue as to how to save the world. I cannot have it on my conscience that Withernsea residents succumbed to some evil force because I'd made the queen stay to do a stock-take. So, sorry, but you're fired," she repeated, in an Alan Sugar's 'The Apprentice' way.

"I think you're having far too much fun sacking me," I huffed.

"Well, I'm sure you'll get over it while you're shopping. You shall continue to qualify for your staff discount."

Indeed, I was over it already; over it and looking around the store. I spotted a short, tight, silver glittery dress that when it moved caught the light and sparkled like a rainbow. "Oh my god, this is perfect."

"Perfect for giving your father a heart attack."

"Dad doesn't have a beating heart, Mum. I'll put that in my trying on pile, Ebs."

***

I had the best time shopping with my mum. As soon as we had heavy bags, we could just whizz off home, drop them off and start all over again. We had a late lunch at Red's Steakhouse and then Mum said goodbye and I made my way to see Alyssa who said she was free.

Her mum let me in. Alyssa was in her bedroom with her earbuds in singing along to *Little Mix*. I knocked on her open door and walked in.

"Hey, Lys."

She pulled the buds out and sat up.

"Hey." She stared at me. "Bloody hell, Charlie, it's

going to take some getting used to seeing you look so different, you know."

I waved a hand in the air. "Oh just pretend I was on *Extreme Makeover* or something."

Her mouth downturned at the corners. "But what are we going to do, Charlie, because the fact is I'm still sixteen and you're what, like early to mid-twenties now? Maybe it'd be better if you looked for a new best friend."

"I don't frikking think so," I told her straight. "Listen, lady. Get what I look like out of your head. I am still completely naive about life. Think of it like I've got the older outside and you've got the older inside. I need your help, bestie."

She sat up straighter. "Well, I guess I did save the pack, so having me in your 'Save Withernsea' arsenal would be advantageous."

"It certainly will. But, babe, right now I need you to explain sex to me, all the ins and outs, and also help me to look my best."

"For a start, maybe you could not describe it as all the ins and outs?"

"Babe, I know nothing. I've never seen a man's bits in real life. No clue what to do with them. Obviously, I know what's supposed to happen, but I mean how do I learn how to be good at it?"

Alyssa put a hand to her brows and covered her eyes. "Jeez." She pulled her laptop from under the bed and placing it on her knee, patted the bed next to her. "I hope my brother doesn't spy on my internet search history after today. We'll start with Pornhub."

In less than a year I'd gone from mashed banana puree to performing a fake blow job on one. From wean to peen.

"That's it, Char, try to get it right to the back of your throat."

The door burst open and Kim walked in, making us jump a foot. She looked disappointed. "Oh, I thought you were having some kind of group sex with the pack and I was going to watch." She sat down on the chair in front of Alyssa's desk. "How disappointing."

"Kim, you can't just burst into my room like that. What about my privacy?" Alyssa complained.

"Privacy? You want to talk to me about privacy? On Friday most of you saw my vagina while I gave birth to three babies."

What could we say to that?

"Anyway, one thing you can take from having to

witness my nether regions is that they were tended to and cared for. There are no weeds growing in my lady-garden. If you're going to be shagging Kai soon you need to get booked in at a salon to ensure everything looks its best."

"I've got a ladyshave. Remember, I was fifteen before. There was hair down there," I reminded her.

"I'm sure Kai is looking forward to getting stubble rash from going down on you," Kim huffed.

"She might have a point," Alyssa said. "Maybe you should go and get things waxed?"

"I'm busy today. Only I need to be back home in two hours so I can be made a wyvern."

Kim took her phone out of her pocket. "Hey there. Can you do a bikini wax? Yeah, come to the main house. Charlie. See you in a few."

She hung up. "Samara's on her way."

My eyes widened. "Samara, the pet groomer?"

Kim shrugged. "Well, you grew overnight. There could be years' worth of hair down there for all I know. She does Afghan's, so you'll be fine."

She stood up. "Right, I'll be back when Samara gets here. In the meantime, I'll go let three babies suckle on me and destroy my great rack." She pointed to the computer. "Might want to search for water sports, so if Kai asks, Char doesn't think he wants to surf. Also, could be a lot of confusion over the subject of diving."

With that she walked out, and the door banged shut behind her.

"That woman," Alyssa exclaimed. "I'll be glad when the cubs are a little older and they move back to their own place. Only right now Mum is insisting on helping. I love my sister-in-law but that's twice she's burst into my room today. She's only been here since late last night. The first time was to ask if I had a vibrator because she'd thought putting it under the bassinet might help Louisa fall to sleep."

I burst out laughing. I loved Kim hard, but she definitely took some getting used to.

"How's it going with Bartholomew?" It was time for the attention to go on my friend. "How did this date come about? I notice *him* being in his twenties isn't a problem for you." I quirked a brow.

She wrinkled her nose. "It kind of is. We went out, and he kept saying things like what do you want to do when you grow up? I told him I'd left school and that I could take a key role within the pack, but he's human. To be honest, I'm not sure how much he understands about the supernatural world. And I can't exactly say 'oh I killed two people and saved the pack, so stop asking me how many GCSE's I got'.

"Anyway, as the evening went on, he relaxed and he started to see that I was indeed a woman and we made out in a shop doorway. But he hasn't asked me out again, and when I saw how he looked at Maisie... well, I kind of think I'm wasting my time."

"How old is he?"

"Twenty."

"He's only four years older than you then, but I guess in terms of experience of both life and sex he could be way ahead of you. You just need to keep reminding him you're a woman, not a girl, and that means not hanging around the coffee shop counter like someone waiting to meet a backstage pop star."

"Yeah, I guess so. Hey, we so need to go clubbing. Oooh, and because you're older, you can help get me in. Oh let's do it later tonight!"

I shook my head. "Alyssa, I'll have had enough today. I don't know what the side effects of becoming a wyvern are yet."

She pouted. "Char, it's Saturday night." She's back on the computer faster than I can say no again. "Look. At ATIK in Hull it's 'Oh la la Saturday'. Free to get in before eleven pm and 50% off drinks. You have your vamp speed so you can get us there in a flash."

"Alyssa, you're always sick when I transport you anywhere."

"Well, I'll probably puke at the end of the night anyway so it's a bit of practice. Pleaassseee? We can let our hair down, get dressed up, and I can try to meet someone who doesn't treat me like I'm a kid."

I sighed rather loudly. "All right. But only because I'm not going to seek out Kai tonight. I want to get used to my new body for a day or so. I want to date him so bad, Lys. But I texted him and said I'd see him on Monday after they formally made me Queen of Wyvern Sea. That gives me two days to get my dad used to the fact I've grown up. I might have to tell him I'm staying over at yours though."

"No problem."

"Do you know?" I told Alyssa. "I reckon saving the world will be like child's play at the side of this adulting lark."

She tilted her head. "How do you prepare for war if you don't know what the threat is, or when it's going to come?"

"I do the only thing I can do. Get as powered up as possible and get on with living my life."

"Samara's here," Kim's voice came floating up the stairs. This was followed by footsteps and then the door opened. "She's waiting for you in the bathroom. I've given her a black sack to collect your bush in. Garden waste strength."

I threw my blue webs out at her and once again a heap flung out rather than just one, coating Kim in what looked like a ball of wool. "I hope that's not a prediction of what's about to happen to Samara," she quipped and left the room.

CHAPTER 6

CHARLIE

After the degradation of a bikini wax performed by a pet groomer, I said a temporary goodbye to Alyssa and arranged to come and fetch her at half past ten to go to the club. Then I made my way back home.

It was just after five and my father met me at the door. He smelled around me. "Good, you don't smell like that sea urchin."

"Theo!" My mum came out into the hallway. "Go and make yourself useful by getting us three bottles of O-neg. Charlie and I could do with being at full strength before we start the process."

"And my strength shall also be full in case I need to assist either of you, yes?"

"No, drinking yours will ensure your mouth is otherwise occupied, as I'm currently fed up of hearing your voice."

"Well, wife, that is quite harsh, but I shall do as I'm bid." My dad put his best sulking face on and stalked out of the room.

My mum threw her hands up in the air exasperated.

After we'd had our drinks, Mum explained she would turn into a wyvern and then would place a hand on my arm which was how my grandad had transferred the powers to her.

"Are you ready? Let's sit on the sofa to do this."

I nodded and made my way to our brand-new sofa.

Mum changed. Her legs grew a lizard skin and wings sprouted from her back. She'd not taken the wings into account when she said sit on the new sofa, and this one wasn't as deep, so she sprang forward. As she did, she clasped my arm and an icy sensation surged through my body. My mum fell on the floor with a thud.

"Ow."

I felt my skin change and jumped up off the sofa. Reptilian skin emerged all over my body. Wings sprouted from my upper back and fins from my lower.

My head felt weird and as I felt at it, the shape of it had changed.

My mum looked at me, her eyes wide. "Oh my god."

"What is it?" I tried to say, but it came out as, "wmoatts hyegret dyat".

"Theoooooo," my mum yelled. Bearing in mind my dad had strong hearing, it wasn't necessary. All it did was send me into a panic. I went to pat my mum and calm her down, but my hands were claws. I screamed and ice-cold water flew out of them freezing my mother in place.

Dad burst in. "What on earth? What have you done to your mother?"

"Dhawwit umbagi jawa."

Dad raised his hand. "Stay very still. I'm ringing your grandfather."

Mary, my other grandma—the ghost one—wafted into the room. "What's happening, Son? Oh look, you've made an ice sculpture of Shelley. How romantic."

"That is Shelley, Mother. Stay with Charlie, will you, while I quickly whizz and get Dylan and Margret?"

"Yes, of course. Do you know where Charlie is?"

she said to me. "Sorry, we've not met. I'm Mary, Theo's dead mother."

"What have I told you about introducing yourself as someone deceased?" my dad said. "And that is Charlie. Something's gone wrong with her wyvern transfer. I'll be back post-haste. No one move."

"Well, Shelley doesn't seem to have much choice, does she?" Mary quipped. "Oh, Charlie, maybe we should have called you Elsa." She started singing 'Let it Go'.

Luckily, within a few minutes my Grandma Margret and Grandad Dylan were here, brought by my dad.

"I told Shelley I would supervise. Just can't get kids to listen these days, can you?" Dylan humphed.

Margret said a spell which thawed out my mother. She stood shivering. "I c-can't g-get w-warm," she complained.

"Come on, love, let's run you a nice hot bath while your dad sorts Charlie out."

"W-what's g-gone wrong?" my mum asked, looking at me with worry etched on her features. I noticed she didn't come any closer though or ask if I was okay.

"It's just teething problems," Grandad said.

"They are rather large and sharp," Dad replied.

Grandad guffawed. "No, not an actual problem with her teeth. She's speaking the old language of the sea, which is seldom used any more. Hopefully, within a few hours, all of this will pass through her system, and she'll return to normal.

A few hours?!!

"My guess is that as she had already used so much energy changing from a teenager to a young woman, it has made this second change take longer than usual."

"She's not going to stay like this then?"

"Oh no, Theo, don't worry. She'll be back to normal before long."

"Shame. She looks really unattractive like this. It would have served to deter the male."

My dad just did not know when to quit.

"Now, Theo." My grandad patted dad on the back. "If I had the same attitude regarding my daughter, you wouldn't be married to her, and there wouldn't be Charlie, would there? You're going to have to accept your daughter will kiss a few frogs to find her prince."

"If she stays like that she might have to marry one of the frogs." My dad burst out laughing.

I growled and held up a hand ready to freeze him.

"Now, now, Charlie," my grandad said. "Your father is only messing with you. No need to freeze anyone else."

God, I was so uncomfortable. I couldn't sit because of the fins and wings. I decided to plod over to the mirror to see what my head looked like. Sure enough, I had the head of a dragon.

"Actually, most females turn into those, wyvern or not," Grandad said to my dad and they burst out laughing again.

Finally, after another hour or so, I felt my body starting to shift. My head returned to its normal shape. My wings and fins disappeared. My claws retracted, and my lizard skin disappeared. I excused myself to go to the bathroom and checked myself over. Yep, I was completely back to normal, thank fuck.

What a day! I was so ready for my bed.

Then I remembered I had to go clubbing yet.

I didn't feel like going clubbing in the slightest, but I had promised Alyssa, and it would take her mind off Bartholomew. Looking through my new clothes, I settled on a plain black dress that covered my knees. I didn't feel like drawing attention to myself tonight. I hoped that as usual, Lys would be made up to the nines and would outshine me and grab all the attention. We had snuck into clubs a couple of times when we were fifteen, but had only stayed for half an hour before we'd had to be home. This was the first night I was attending properly as an adult, and Lys was sixteen now, so as far as I was concerned it was near enough to eighteen. It wasn't like she had school the next morning or anything. The woman had saved her pack and killed two rogue weres, so it would have been a little churlish to tell her she wasn't old enough to go to a club.

I whizzed over to find her wearing a red PVC dress, with matching ankle boots that laced up her legs. Her door was blocked by one angry werewolf brother who currently had tufts of hair sprouting out from around his neck showing that at any given point he was about to go full-on were.

"You are not setting one foot outside this house dressed like that, little sister," he snarled, jumping as I appeared.

"Bloody hell, Charlie. I'll never get used to you vamps just whizzing in. Tell her about her outfit, will you?"

Great. Piggy in the middle. How to play it? Well, there was one thing. It was good for practicing diplomacy in getting ready for war.

"Lys, Chica. We don't match. Have you got your glitter gold dress and matching wedges? I thought I could borrow your gold glitter belt to go with this dress and then we'd co-ordinate." I wafted myself. "You look hot though, babe. No one would give me a second look if you wore that. We'd be beating them off with a stick. In fact, you'd look too hot, we wouldn't get to chat."

I watched my friend's face change expressions as she debated all this with herself. She got up in her brother's face. "I'm getting changed, but only because I want to co-ord with my bestie. You don't get to tell me what to do."

"Actually, I do because I'm the Alpha—"

I broke into a fake coughing fit loud enough to interrupt him as I cried, "Water."

Darius rushed out of the room, presumably to get me a drink.

"Hurry up and get changed and let's get out of here before he gets back," I told her. Two minutes later we were gone. Darius would return to an empty room.

The nightclub was all brick walls and wooden floors. It stretched over four storeys. I'd booked us a booth right near the dance floor, so we had somewhere to chill and chat. I could have whizzed us straight inside but had to do things the proper way to get directed to our booth, so we waited outside in a queue for fifteen minutes first. It gave us a chance to chat normally before we would end up shouting to be heard over the top of the music.

"I'm really excited about tonight," I told my friend. "After all the stress of late, I'm ready to let my hair down metaphorically speaking. Let's go for it and get crazy drunk."

"Whoa! Who is this Charlie and what have you done with my friend? Hell yeah! I agree," she told me.

Looking further back in the queue I spotted Bartholomew. I stared at Alyssa. "Did you tell Sir Loins we were coming?"

"Yeah, he asked me if I wanted to meet him at McDonalds. Fucking McDonalds! I told him I was coming here with you. Stupid twat. He really needs an education in the fact I'm a woman and not a bloody kid."

"Well, don't look around but he's in the queue."

Her eyes widened. "You're joking?"

"No, I'm not. And with the way he's undressing you with his eyes right now, I think he can see you for exactly who you are."

"Well, I'm here tonight with you. Ho's before bro's, so he can sod off."

"I don't mind if in a bit you want to go off with him. I can whizz home as long as I know he's going to make sure you get home safely."

"No. No one asked him to come here tonight. This evening is about me, you, and alcohol." At that point we entered the building, found our booth, and bought the first of what would be a large amount of gin.

"This purple is such a beaauuuutiful colour. Who knew you could have pretty purple gin?" Alyssa slurred. We'd been dancing the night away. Bartholomew had come straight over when he'd got inside and had got short shrift from Alyssa who told him she was out with me. He'd apparently told her how hot she looked. He was currently on the dance floor with a redhead, no doubt trying to make Lys jealous, but we were too drunk to care.

"It's pathetic. Men are pathetic, aren't they? I don't think I rate Bart anymore."

"Bart Simpson. What a name. Bahahahahaha. Come on, let's go and dance at the side of them and completely ignore him."

We moved onto the floor where we orchestrated a series of sexy dance moves. At one point Bart was so entranced in Alyssa's moves that he stopped dancing and just stared.

Two men moved closer to us on the dance floor

and one started dancing in front of me, standing in between me and my bestie. It was annoying, but I figured what the hell, I may as well enjoy myself, so I raised my arms above my head and swung my body to the music. The guy moved in closer. I didn't want him to hit on me, I only wanted Kai, but I was here with Alyssa, and nothing had started with Kai yet, so I figured a dance didn't hurt. I turned around so my back was to him and did a sultry up and down kind of wiggle like I'd seen on TV. When I looked back around, the guy wasn't there anymore. I searched around, a crease between my brows and then noticed Alyssa's finger pointing to a wall at the other side of the club where the man was slumped against it while his friend pushed his way through the crowd in a panic to get to him.

"How the hell did he get—"

"Your dad," Alyssa said. "Seriously, it's like I imagined it because it was so fast. One minute the guy was there, the next he was hitting that wall."

I sighed. "And where is my dad now?" My eyes scanned the room before returning to Alyssa.

She shrugged her shoulders. "He disappeared as fast as he appeared."

"I'm going to kill him. He must be following me."

"Babes, you didn't want that guy anyway, and he

was about to hit on you at any minute. Your dad did you a favour. Let's get another drink and go back to the booth."

I was too drunk to protest. My bloody father though! I'd be having words with him tomorrow. When I could think more clearly and speak without slurring. My mum would have to sort him out. The guy was out of control.

"Don't look, Lys. Bart is standing at the top of our booth with that girl. She's all laughing and twirling her hair, and she keeps looking daggers over here. It's ridiculous. Hasn't she any self-respect? He's basically eye-fucking you every five seconds. I'd ditch his arse."

"And he acts like I'm the child." Lys knocked back another vodka. "Fuck this. I'm going to sort this out." She stood up, wobbling slightly to one side and then made her way over to them both. Because I'd inherited great hearing from my vamp father, I could hear everything without having to move.

"Bartholomew, baby. Why are you standing at the edge of the booth when you know you can come sit alongside me?" Lys pouted, completely ignoring the woman at the side of him.

Bart looked wrongfooted. "I- erm... sorry... Li-, erm, Rihanna."

"My name's Lianne," the woman shouted, and

with that she stomped off back over to her friends. I didn't need to hear her conversation, given the mutinous look on her face as she spoke to her mates, to guess what she was saying.

"Shucks. I just remembered. It's girls' night, so you can't come into the booth after all. Sorry, Bart," she told him.

"It's Bartholomew." Bart went on the defensive over his name.

"I can't say that when I'm drunk." Alyssa swayed. "Bye, Bart. I don't like men who play games. You want to date me? Impress me. Don't try to make me jealous. It doesn't work. It just makes me see you as a sad tosser."

She came back to sit next to me. "I've had enough now, Char. Can we go? I've had a great time, but these people are spoiling it. Anyway, I'm starving. Can we have chips?"

We left the bar, unaware of where Bart had gone to, or my father's current whereabouts. We followed the smell of food which took us down an alleyway near the club.

"Hey, bitch. You don't move in on my man like that. You get me?"

We turned around. It was the girl from the club and her mates. She had a glass in her hand full of drink.

Oh shit. She and her three friends moved closer. I heard a growl in Alyssa's throat. There was currently no one else around so if she changed we were okay, but I tried to calm her.

"We're going for chips, Lys. Don't change. She's not worth it."

I held up a hand at the women. "The guy's her ex. He doesn't know when to go away."

"Why did she come over then? If she'd stayed in her seat, I'd have still been with him right now."

"Are you sure about that?" I asked her. "Because from where I was looking, he spent half the night with his eyes on my best mate. Maybe you should rate yourself better than to hang around with a guy who clearly wants someone else."

The contents of the drink coated me as it got flung in my face. I felt the water against my skin and an icy sensation hit my system. "Oh shit."

In a flash, scales crept up my skin, my wings sprouted, and my dragon head appeared. Being drunk I just thought 'fuck it', and I roared in the direction of the women, who screamed for dear life and ran away from the alley.

I burst into peals of laughter and then the next thing I knew, I was whizzed away. I vaguely remembered dropping Alyssa off to an angry Darius and then seeing my own bed.

I woke with a pounding headache. God, it had been an awesome night. But how had I got home? Leaving the club was a complete blur.

At the side of my bed, I found a glass of water and two painkillers, along with a note.

Figured you'd need these
Love, Dad xo

I remembered then about him flinging my dance partner across the bar and him appearing in the alleyway. Oh Lord. I'd turned into a wyvern in the middle of Hull! How could I be mad at him when he'd saved me from exposing myself as a supernatural to people who didn't know we existed?

I sighed and slumped back against my pillow as it hit me that as queen, my life was not my own. In order to keep the residents of Withernsea safe, I would have to watch my behaviour and restrict my boundaries. Because I couldn't do what I did last night—get so drunk, I wasn't in control of myself where I could put people in danger.

It was at that point I began to realise just what a burden and responsibility being queen was going to be.

CHAPTER 7

SHELLEY

I needed to have a stern word with my husband. There was being an overprotective parent and then there was stalking your own daughter. Things came to a head when I walked in to find him watching a live surveillance feed of her wandering down to the chip shop that evening.

"Theo. Enough. This has got to stop. She needs her privacy."

"Shelley. She is prophesied to save Withernsea. What if someone tries to kill her?" His face was so earnest. It reminded me of just how much I loved him, but his behaviour still had to be curtailed.

I sat beside him and placed a hand on his arm, giving it a squeeze. "Theo, I know. I worry about her too, but we would anyway. Just as any parent worries about their child. But you have to back off or she will turn away from you altogether. She still has her life to lead, and she has to do that *independently*. She will be dating, and she will be sleeping with men, Theo." His eyes flashed red, and his fangs descended.

I gave him a moment to recover himself.

"Turn the surveillance off and take the camera off our daughter. Get the bed and breakfast up and running. You need something to occupy your time and we have another hundred years before we can make another baby."

Theo looked up at me. "You'd want another?"

"Wouldn't you?"

He shrugged his shoulders. "I don't know. All this worry that comes with it. I can't settle. I'm not sure I can go through all that again."

I half-smiled. "Well, there's plenty of time to think about it, and I don't mind either way. We might get a grandchild soon anyway and we can hand those back."

The fangs were back. When would I learn?

"She could get pregnant? To that sea urchin? I'd not even considered that." He held his chin and looked furtive. "I need to try to get hold of some of his DNA. Make sure he has a good heritage."

I scrubbed a hand down my face. "Theo. There

will be no surveillance, no getting hold of DNA, and no stalking. You back off now, okay?"

He sighed a heavy sigh. "If I must."

"Where is the camera on Charlie?"

"It's in the button on her jacket. I'll remove it when she gets back."

"I'll be keeping an eye on you, Theo, to make sure temptation doesn't get in your way and you start spying again."

His face took on a mischievous glint. "Well, wife. I think you should put other temptations in my way and then I shall be completely distracted and have no time to worry about what our daughter is doing."

"Hmmm, I guess we are still kind of in our own honeymoon period," I told him, switching off the monitors, and giving my husband something else to focus on.

Monday morning rolled around and Jax had set up a meeting at ten am of the *Female Entrepreneurs do it with their Colleagues* group, so we all descended on the coffee shop ready to talk upcoming business plans. I was very surprised on entering to find my adoptive father in the shop nursing a hot drink. In fact, it was that hot, steam was billowing out of the top. Don't tell me the machine was playing up, I'd be suicidal. "Mark?" I'd stopped calling them mum and dad lately, as I didn't feel they'd earned it anymore, and I now had my real parents around.

"Hey, Shelley."

"Erm, what brings you here this morning? Not that it isn't nice to see you," I lied.

"Your mum insisted that I make the effort to come and say hello. She's right. I need to spend more time with you girls."

"Okay, well, Polly's not here."

"Oh, I know. She called and told me she'd moved. Most daughters who travel go overseas not under it. It's all a bit much to take in to be honest with you. Anyway, I thought I'd just pop in for a quick brew on my way to work."

"You live and work in Hull. This is rather out of the way, isn't it?"

"Well, maybe your mum and I will move to Withernsea and look for work here. Food for thought."

Oh God no!

He looked at me strangely and I hoped I'd not said that out loud.

"So, what's new with you and yours? Took on any more powers? Killed any bad guys?"

"Just running my dating agency and raising my daughter like any other normal parent."

"But you're not, are you? A normal parent? Your daughter grew to the size of a twenty-year-old in months."

He was starting to piss me off.

"Yes, well prepare yourself because it could be a sign that the war in Withernsea is upon us. Seems whether you phoned the press or not, war is coming."

"I do apologise for that. It was a rash move. Has Charlene become even more powerful by the way? Developed any new superpowers?"

"Her strength increases every day. Thanks for asking about her wellbeing," I said sarcastically. "If you're interested, I took her to the caves and they say she's fine. The change hasn't caused her any difficulties." I noted my friends were waiting for me. "Well, it was—" I stopped. I couldn't tell him it was nice to see him because it wasn't. "Erm, have a good day at work."

"Thanks. I'm sure I will. Being here has been a delightful start to it." He left his drink and the coffee shop.

"What was that all about?" Jax asked me as I took a seat at the table.

"I have no idea, but I'd hazard a guess that Debbie has forced him to come because he didn't exactly exude remorse for his previous behaviour. Typical that Polly wasn't here. She's related by blood, she should have to put up with him." I took a large swig of the coffee placed in front of me. "I need this more than ever today. In fact, I could do with a spa day. I'm bloody fed up and could do with a complete day off from everything. My brain needs a holiday."

"I'll come with you, but only if you sign a statement guaranteeing you waxed," Samara told me. She crinkled her nose as if there was a bad smell under it.

"Is this to do with my daughter? Kim said you'd been doing maintenance."

"Oh no." Samara waved a hand. "She was fine. No, we had a team building day for Humber and the East yesterday, and oh my fucking god, we gathered around the table supposedly to eat a healthy lunch after being in the sauna, and Rebecca from Hornsea realised she needed glasses."

My brow furrowed. "What has someone's eyesight got to do with waxing?"

"She didn't realise she'd missed trimming most of her pubes. There they were on display out of both sides of her swimsuit, and lo and behold they'd put black seaweed on the table as part of the lunch. I felt like I was eating her bush." She made a gagging impression. "Anyway, I *may* have asked her to close her legs and it *may* have drawn everyone's attention to it. Basically, she swore revenge on me. Said I was a fake and a cheat, that I was helped by the dating agency, and she would draw attention to my failings as I had hers. I don't know why she was so upset. I was the one who had to endure my eyeballs being assaulted. Anyway, I'll go with you because obviously I tensed up after seeing that, so I could do with another sesh."

"And what did you say to her threats?" Jax asked.

"I told her to shut her mouth... and her legs."

"I think I'll take a raincheck on the spa day for now. Just until we know Withernsea is free from the risk of war," I said, as it didn't sound like it was going to be much of a relaxing experience if I took Samara with me.

At that point the door opened, and Ebony came in.

"Sorry, I'm a little late. Had a customer."

"Oh yeah, did you give them what they wanted, Eb? Fulfil that customer's every desire?" Samara winked. "Did you have a *brush* with fate? Are you free of white *paint* splatters?"

"It was a real customer. Now turn your phone off because I saw in a vision that Kim would call you and feed you these very lines to me."

Samara rolled her eyes and pressed the speaker-phone on. "She rumbled you, babe."

"That bloody seer."

"Why have you got Samara being your ventriloquist's dummy?" I shouted near the phone.

"Because I wanted to be with you guys, but I couldn't get away today. My pussy is so sore." The other customers in the coffee shop's heads swivelled around at super speed. "Take her off loudspeaker." I waved at Samara. "Then pass me the phone."

"Kim. You are on maternity leave. Now be with your babies. I'm ending the call." I placed the phone face down on the table. "Okay, can we finally get to talking about some business? What's everyone got coming up?"

"I need a replacement for Charlie in the boutique so I'm going to ask Alyssa. She assisted Charlie while I was on honeymoon. Do you think Charlie would be offended that I sacked her and took on her friend?"

I sighed. "Charlie has a lot to get used to. It's going to be a tricky time for her. No, I'd hope she'd be happy for her friend."

"Did I hear Lys might be working next door?" Bartholomew had wandered over.

"I've not asked her yet, so I'd appreciate it if you could not mention what you just overheard," Ebony told him with a look that could have cut glass. "You will learn. Alyssa is a warrior. She needs a man who can support her strengths. You are not worthy," she said in the strange 'voice from the fates' tone she got occasionally.

His mouth dropped open.

"Ooh, sorry about that. Wasn't expecting it," Ebony apologised as if she'd accidently burped, not blurted out seer stuff.

"We've got customers, Bartholomew. If you wouldn't mind serving them while I'm over here. *Like I pay you to,*" Jax muttered under her breath.

"Trouble?" I asked her.

She sighed. "Not really, but first I've had Alyssa hanging around the shop and now he's mooning around wondering if she's getting a job next door. He's here to work, not to sort out his dating life. The agency is upstairs."

"Just you remember that before you got together with Tristan, you employed Bartholomew because he was hot."

She stuck her tongue out at me. "Fair point well made. Now stick this in your mouth." She shoved a chocolate doughnut in my direction. I intercepted it and begrudgingly put it back on the plate for a moment.

"Now, there's something I want to talk to you all about while a certain someone is in the office."

The others gave me their attention.

"If you aren't aware of it yet, Lucy and Frankie married while they were on their travels." I waited for their expressions to register shock at my gossip.

No one looked surprised.

"You all knew?"

"Saw it in a vision," Ebony said.

"Well, I think we need a celebration to cheer us all up and take our mind off possible upcoming events, so I thought we'd throw them a wedding reception. I thought a week on Friday? Could we hold it here, Jax? Just invite a few people who they know well?"

"Yes, of course. I'll do a buffet for it." Jax smiled.

"I'll trim the place up," Samara added. "With lots of hearts and flowers."

"I'll offer the bride the chance to choose a dress for the reception," Ebony said.

"I'll get Maisie to let me into their house so I can decorate their bedroom with rose petals for when they get home," I added.

"Does Lucy know you're doing this?" Jax asked.

"Yes. She's finally come around to the idea. The words 'present list' worked amazingly."

"And where is this present list? On Amazon?"

"Yes, check out the wish list under HotStuff-Withernsea."

Jax keyed it into her mobile phone. "There are only Tom Hardy DVDs on her list."

"She said I can borrow them, so I had no objections to buying her a couple," I said.

"Well, if she's sharing, I'll buy her a couple too," added Jax.

"We might have to change the name of this group to the 'Tom Hardy Appreciation Society', I joked. I saw Jax's face fall. God, she was sensitive.

"I'm joking. Our name is brilliant," I reassured her. "Okay, I'd better get some work done. We're off to see the duke tonight for Charlie to become Queen of Wyvern Sea."

Ebony sniggered.

"What?" I asked her. "Have you seen something?"

"Might have," she said and she wouldn't tell me anything else.

And she called herself my friend!

CHAPTER 8

CHARLIE

I'd enjoyed a quiet day yesterday recovering from my hangover and finishing up with a gorgeous chip supper seeing as the night before's had been scuppered by jealous women. Today, seeing as I no longer had a job at Ebony's boutique, I decided to have a pamper day and slowly get ready for my under the sea coronation and the fact that afterward I would meet Kai. We were going to have a meal at his place. Oh my! Would tonight be the night?

To say I was nervous was an understatement. I wasn't convinced that an education from Pornhub was the way to go and so last night I'd gone on some forums on the internet for advice. I'd ended up reading several horror stories about broken penises and now I wasn't sure I'd be able to relax enough to do anything.

Anyway, I was getting ahead of myself. We'd not even had a date yet.

By the time my mum came home from work and my dad had got up from his vampire slumber, I was polished and preened to within an inch of my life. I'd painted my nails in a range of pastel metallics: pink, blue, green; and my hair was tied back in a plait. I knew part of the ceremony was dumping seawater on my head, so I'd figured a plait would ensure I stayed tidy after a soaking.

I stared at myself in the mirror in the hallway before we left. This was the final stage in preparation. I'd be Queen Charlene of Wyvern Sea when I returned.

My mum came up behind me. "Are you okay, Charlie?"

"Yeah. Let's go."

We were picked up at the beach as usual. My dad had insisted that Grandad Dylan and Grandma Margret come as they could help if there were any problems. Then strangely we were also accompanied by Debbie and Mark, my other 'grandparents', who had insisted to Shelley over the telephone that they wanted to be involved as they were so proud. Yeah, right. I knew

Debbie was trying to make amends for the past, but it all seemed too little, too late. However, because Polly and Drake would be there and so they could visit them too, Mum hadn't felt able to say no. My dad's mother, Mary, was currently in a sulk as she couldn't travel underwater as a ghost.

Mark and Debbie held onto each other tightly as the boat sped under the sand and when we reappeared next to the Duke's home he had his hand on her butt. They'd been touchy feely since we'd met them at the beach, and it was making me a little nauseous.

My mum was carrying her crown in a box. On land it looked rusted, but under the water it sparkled with its gemstones. She placed it on her head before descending and we exited the boat. Duke Brishon stood outside his home, dressed in a silver shell-suit that clung around his large belly, and ceremonial gold chains around his neck. He looked like a pimp. Mum acknowledged the duke's bow with a nod of her own head.

"Welcome, Your Highness, and guests. Please come inside where we shall perform the ceremony and have some refreshments. I felt the town hall would be a little too formal, for are we not almost family now?" He nodded towards Drake and Polly who came running from the living room out into the hallway to greet us.

"Hey, sis, niece." Polly smiled a huge beaming smile. Then again, she'd won her man on Friday and had no doubt been celebrating ever since so she could be forgiven her smug look. Then the smile disappeared as she saw our extra guests. "Oh, Mum and Dad. This is a surprise."

"We would have called but we preferred to catch you unawares. Surprise you. More fun that way, eh, sweetie?" said Mark. No way was I calling him grandad.

"We thought you could give us a tour of your new home and of course we're here to celebrate. It's not every day your grandaughter becomes queen is it?" Debbie said.

"Your own daughter was queen. You didn't seem to care then?" Polly shot out.

"Yes, yes. We made many mistakes, and we apologise and are determined to do our best to atone for them. We were very proud of you too, Shelley," Debbie added.

Mark's eyes took in everything around him. Like he was imprinting it in his mind. I didn't trust him. The guy had threatened to go to the press just days ago, and now mum had let him come underwater? I would mention it later, but for now, I needed this ceremony over with so I could meet Kai.

After a drink and some canapes, we made our way out onto the duke's rear patio.

"Please tell me that this time I don't get covered in dirty seawater," my mum said.

"No. No," The duke replied.

Mum's shoulders visibly relaxed.

"No, you have to be coated in fish excrement for the handover."

"I beg your pardon, but did you just say fish shit?" my mum spat out. "Because that's not happening."

The duke shrugged. "Without it the handover cannot take place. You'll just have to stay queen then."

Mum looked to the heavens and then at Drake. "Is this true, Drake, and not something your father's made up in retaliation for us stopping the wedding on Friday?"

"Queen, you wound me. And while I will enjoy every minute, I swear it is part of the ritual. It does have skin firming properties. Alas these—"

"Let me guess, can only be seen under the water, or they'd be pilfered by those above."

"My queen, you have learned our ways, just before you leave your post. You shall be a good advisor to your daughter. Now, shall we?" He pointed to the arbour erected on the patio.

And so we all watched as my mum was smeared all over her face and neck in a dark paste.

"Dear God, even magic does not smell this bad," my dad said, earning himself a death glare from my mum.

"I now dissolve you of your position as queen," Duke Brishon told her, removing her crown and passing it to Drake to hold. "Princess Charlene, if you could step forward."

I stood under the arbour desperately trying to hold my breath.

"Okay, please kneel."

I did as asked. In the end I'd decided to dress in a plain grey trouser suit with a black top. I figured it would hide most of the marks from dirty seawater.

"In front of these gathered witnesses, I bestow upon Charlene Kimberly Landry the rule of Wyvern Sea. I grant her access to the waters, and safe passage to her and anyone she may choose to travel alongside her to visit us in the future. All of the sea bows to thee, our new queen. Do you accept this position? If so, please accept now in front of these witnesses."

This was it. "I accept the position of Queen of Wyvern Sea."

Drake placed the jewelled crown upon my head and Brishon told me to stand. "The people of the sea will wish to pledge their allegiance to you, so if you could come with me and stand outside my home."

I followed him back through his doorway to be greeted by a myriad of different sea creatures who bowed in front of me before swimming away.

Finally, Brishon held in front of me a golden box covered in pictures of fish. I knew what was coming. The dirty seawater. I'd seen it at our house when Mum had been made the queen. Brishon opened the box and threw the contents at me. Fish shaped pink confetti floated out over me.

"What the actual fuck?" Mum shouted. "Where's the dirty seawater?"

Brishon shrugged. "It only takes on that appearance outside of the sea. Under the water it is confetti."

"But I still had to be coated in fish shit? What happens if Charlie is no longer queen? Will she get coated in fish shit, or will it have changed to *Creme De La Mer* by then? I'm going to find a bathroom." She stomped off in a huff. Anyone would have thought she wanted me to be coated in crap!

"And that concludes the ceremony. Let us applaud Queen Charlene of Wyvern Sea."

The people around us clapped, and my father took me in his arms and gave me a huge hug. "Daughter, I am very proud of you. I will shortly gather all your relatives and take them back to land. I would guess you are staying awhile?"

He nodded over to a few hundred feet away, where Kai stood waiting for me.

"I know you find it hard, Dad, but thank you."

He sighed. "Can you find other words than hard when talking about boyfriends, Charlie? And believe me when I tell you it is taking considerable inner strength to not walk over to him and threaten him within an inch of his life."

I laughed. "I think Kai is already crystal clear on that one. Now take Mum home, get her washed up, praise her youthful looks and take her out to dinner because otherwise she is going to turn from stinking smell wise, to being in a stinker of a mood."

"Already made the booking at Hanif's. See you later... Queen." He bowed, smiled, and moved away.

Leaving me with Kai.

CHAPTER 9

CHARLIE

My eyes met Kai's beautiful green gaze and the rest of the sea ceased to exist. I looked him over, drinking him in. He'd cut his red hair, and it was now short at the sides and longer on top. My fingers ached to run through it. His merman tail swished, showing a myriad of iridescent scales in shades of blue and green. His pale torso was ripped and toned. Holy moly. I felt like I was going to collapse at the knees at any moment. He swam towards me.

"Charlie. Well, you were lovely before, but now I can't sum up how beautiful you look tonight." He tipped his head. "The crown suits you."

My hands shot up to it. "Oh yes, my crown. I'd totally forgotten." I giggled nervously. "Shall I take it off?"

"No, you are queen of the sea. I will take you to my home and we shall store it safely while we eat. There would be many under the water who would like it as an ornament in their home, so always wear it. It cannot be stolen from your head. Watch."

He leaned over to try to take it, but it wouldn't move. A beaming smile came over his face. "See. Magic."

His hand fell down to my face and grazed my cheek. I shivered under his touch.

"Shall we go?" he said, and I nodded.

He held out his hand. I took it, and then we were on our way through the water, though under the sea you could not feel its presence, you just knew it was there. His tail wiggled as we moved through the water, and I made the most of our hands being entwined. We approached a small stone cottage, and he dropped down to the sand floor where his tail became legs, clad as usual in sparkly scale-patterned leggings that belonged in a 1970's disco. We were going to have to do something about his wardrobe choices for when he came ashore. Maybe it was time Ebony expanded into a small line of menswear? I laughed to myself. I bet he was thinking the same thing about my own wardrobe choices, wondering how he could gently tell me I needed a seashell bikini.

"What's funny?"

"I was just wondering what I should be wearing underwater, like a seashell bikini or something."

The charge between us picked up in voltage. We were about to fry the sea if we didn't calm things down a little. We weren't even through his doorway yet.

"Before we go in." Those green eyes were back on mine. "Nothing's going to happen tonight, Charlie, other than us getting to know each other better."

My face must have shown my disappointment.

"I'd like nothing more than to take you straight to my bed and us not surface for years." He tipped my chin up with his fingers, so I was forced to look at him. "But I will treat my queen with respect, and I mean my queen, as in my beautiful lady, not your role as queen of the sea. Tonight, I will show you my cooking skills; another night..." He winked. "Some other ones."

Between my legs pulsed at the intimation of what he was going to teach me.

"Now." He offered me a crooked elbow. "Would you like a tour of my humble abode?"

I nodded and we walked through the doorway where he pointed to a small table in the hallway where I could put my crown. From there we went into an open plan living and dining room. Much of the furniture was made from driftwood, and the cottage had the whole beach theme about it, painted in blues, whites, and greys. I felt instantly at home. I loved it.

Gorgeous aromas permeated the house: tomatoes, chocolate. My mouth watered and this time it wasn't due to Kai.

"I'm not showing you the kitchen, or you'll get a sneak peek of dinner. While I'm fixing it, why don't you go and wander upstairs and have a look at the rest of the cottage?" he suggested.

I nodded, making my way to the staircase and wandering upstairs. Firstly, I walked into the bathroom. A massive white sunken tub was the focus in the middle of the large bathroom. The floor surrounding the bath was the most stunning cerulean blue, and the walls were a similar shade. If you were in the tub you'd feel like you were in the sea itself.

"Press the button on the wall," Kai shouted upstairs. I found it and pressed it. The walls developed images of fish traveling around in shoals. I watched enraptured for a few minutes and then turning it off, I walked back along the hallway into another room. This one was a study. There was a driftwood desk with a matching chair, although the chair was cushioned for comfort. Sketchbooks were scattered over the desk containing design after design. The fact I'd never asked Kai what he did made me realise just how much we had to learn about each other. He was right to suggest we waited before we became more intimate. Firstly, I needed to know him: his mind, his likes and dislikes. I'd only skimmed the surface of the man I was convinced was my true love. Had my intuition been nothing but a fifteen-year-old girl's crush? I didn't think so, but the evening would be a chance to learn more about Kai, the person.

I left the room, entering the last room upstairs and finding myself in Kai's bedroom. Driftwood fronted wardrobes lined the back wall, and his headboard was a stunning piece of it. The rest of the room was in greys. It was plain, but he had a large woven throw on the bed that looked just the thing to wrap yourself in on a winter's night.

You want to wrap yourself in Kai, not a blanket.

Smiling, I left the room and made my way downstairs. Kai was sitting on the sofa. He rose as I returned.

"Your home is beautiful, Kai."

"Thank you."

"Did you make all the furniture?"

"I did. That's my job. I have a workshop out the back. I love my work, making beauty out of the sea's natural resources."

"Well, it looks amazing. I'm going to tell my mum and dad about it. I bet my mum would love some of those kind of pieces in the farmhouse. I'm guessing these do look the same on land?"

"They do. I considered taking on some apprentices and making more pieces to sell ashore. Something to think about in the future. For now, please take a seat at the table and I shall serve our dinner."

I took my seat at the small circular dining table in the corner of the room. Kai brought out a fish terrine.

"Do you not feel like you're eating your friends?" I asked.

He shook his head. "For the queen of the sea you have much to learn. But don't worry, I will teach you. We have our underwater species, and we have fish and plants for eating, plus underwater vegetables; just as you grow plants ashore and have cows in your fields. We don't think you make friends with the cows and don't eat them, although I have heard of people who don't eat meat."

"Of course. How stupid of me to think every single thing under the sea was a species of sea-folk." I sighed. "Why on earth have I been made queen? The role should have gone to someone who lives under the sea and who knows all about it."

"You can learn, Charlie. And you are impartial. The people under here either have no interest in the politics of the sea, or they are too deeply entrenched in years of bitter wrangling."

The mouthful of terrine soon distracted me from the woes and worries of being queen as I made a bunch of embarrassing noises focused around how amazing this food was and how it tantalised my taste buds.

"Oh my god, Kai, you can cook. This is phenomenal. If the rest of dinner is like this, how do you expect me to ever be satisfied by anything ashore ever again?"

"Then my mission will have been accomplished. To keep you permanently satisfied here under the sea," he told me. I was glad I was sitting as my legs turned to jelly once more. "Also, while I am glad you're enjoying my food, if you continue to make those noises I'm not sure I can keep to my vow of getting to know you first."

I laughed. "Sorry, but it's all your fault. It's just too delicious."

"Like the person eating it. I'll go get the second course," he said, then he looked down at his trousers. "Erm, in a moment."

We both burst out laughing. Standing, I picked up the dishes. "I'll be clearing away while we wait."

I hovered by the table. "Hmm, I thought you might protest about me clearing up; that I might spoil seeing things in the kitchen..."

He looked at me, blowing his fringe away from his face. "Kind of might help my 'situation' if you're not near me for a minute."

That made me break out in hearty guffaws.

"Aw, it's just a stiffy. No hard feelings."

He raised an eyebrow, and giggling, I walked through to the kitchen.

Through his kitchen window I could see the back door led out to a workshop, and there were pieces of work-in-progress around including the most beautiful bench seat. The man was truly talented.

He came into the kitchen. "Okay, please take a seat again so I can bring out the main courses. I'm fine now."

"I was just looking at your wood." His eyes widened, and he quickly looked down.

"Outside." I winked.

"You're incorrigible, Miss Landry."

The main course was pasta and some gorgeous herby kind of sauce. Kai did tell me the name, but I forgot. I was too busy staring at him to be honest.

"How does it feel to you, to now be in your twenties when you were just around fifteen? What's your mind like?"

"Do you mean am I still infantile from my fast progression to adulthood? I feel like I am and have always been in my twenties. Like the previous bit didn't happen. Earlier, I could still feel remnants of being a teen, but it's gone. It's so very strange. I guess it's even more unusual to you?" I bit my lip.

"No. That's what's so weird. It's like you've always been like this to me too. Like I've known you for years. It's so difficult to describe. Only a few days ago you were the teenage Charlie and I felt bad for being attracted to you. Now it's like everything is as it should be."

"I don't know what my future holds, Kai." I mopped my lip with a napkin. "There's no knowing how I will age, or even if I'm supposed to survive the war. You need to be aware of this."

Kai shrugged. "I just have a gut feeling it will all be okay. That we're destined. It's always seemed that way."

"And to me," I told him. "I guess we can only hope that's the way it goes."

We spent the rest of the evening eating chocolate torte and asking each other many, many questions and then Kai called for Daniel to take me back to shore.

We stood in the living room next to the door and said goodbye. Kai's arms wrapped around me and he pulled me close. His hand went into my hair, and he tilted my head up to his. His lips met mine and a thousand fireworks went off in my body. I didn't want him to let me go. I didn't want to go home. Our tongues tangled as our mouths moved together in sweet harmony. It was Kai who broke the kiss. I think I would have still been there hours later if he hadn't.

"Goodnight, my beautiful queen. He picked my crown up from the sideboard next to the doorway and fixed it back on top of my no doubt ruffled hair.

"When will I see you again?" I asked, annoyed that I sounded so needy, but wanting to know.

"Well, that is down to you because I don't know your 'saving the world' timetable, but for me, every single day or night that you have free, I want you to spend it with me. You can watch me work, and we can get to know each other further."

"I'm sure you'd like some time to yourself."

"If I have the choice of time to myself or time with you, then you win every time. Now get in that boat because in a minute I'm not letting you go."

It was a tough choice. I was so tempted to stay. But I made my way to Daniel and before long I was back in my own bed where I had the most wonderful night's dreams about a guy with beautiful green eyes.

CHAPTER 10

SHELLEY

"Shelley, Theo. How wonderful. Come, come, take a seat." Rav seemed thoroughly overexcited this evening.

"Hey, Rav. You're jolly. Have you had too many energy drinks again? Been drinking on an evil guy's life force?"

"No. It's just tonight has been very quiet apart from one irritating customer and you two are just the entertainment I need. I mean your first date." Rav mimed throwing food. "It was hilarious. Theo, if you had been allergic to garlic you would have just burned right here in the restaurant. People would have thought it was like a fire-eater act gone wrong. I can't wait to see what tonight brings."

"We're married now, Rav. I'm sure we're unlikely to provide the same level of entertainment."

Rav sighed. "True, Shelley. Most married couples say nothing at all and just stare into space. They sigh a lot, eat, and then get the bill. Now you have spoiled my evening. Sit wherever you like. I shall still however get you some complimentary poppadoms."

Taking a seat, I raised an eyebrow at my husband. "We need to get Rav a wife, Theo. I'm surprised he left the agency's books."

"His mother wishes to sort out his wife, and also with him being a demon, he's basically decided he's impossible to find a partner for. He says if the demon thing doesn't put them off, his mother will."

"Hmm. I shall have a think about that one. They need to be able to not be scared of demons or demon mother-in-laws. Do you know, I might have just the person," I told Theo. "Leave it with me."

"Good luck with that one. I met Neelam, Rav's mother, once. She cut my hair. Actually cut my hair while I was at her house. Said I'd let it grow too long and should be ashamed of myself. Then she gave me three carrier bags full of home-cooked Indian food because I needed feeding up. She couldn't get on with the whole concept of me drinking only blood. Said there was no wonder I was so slim if I'd got myself on a liquid-only diet."

"So his mum is human? Lucy said he had demon parents."

"Demonic father, human mother. She just said she thought his father had a bit of a temper and so she'd thrown him out when Rav was younger. I tell you, she's a match for any demon that woman. I hope you know what you're doing, sending some poor female in her path."

"Well, like I said. I'll give it some thought, but I do think Rav could do with some love in his life."

Theo grasped my hand over the table. "My beautiful wife, always thinking of other people's love and happiness."

"It is kind of my job, but when I think of how happy we are, I want that for everyone. I hate the thought of there being war, Theo, and our daughter being in the middle of it all. Why can't people just love one other?"

"I know. Believe me I have lived through many difficult times."

"Gosh, yes, I bet you have."

"Such as when Charlene left *Neighbours*. I didn't get out of bed for a month."

I was interrupted from tutting by Rav. "Your poppadoms. Are you ready to order?"

"Rav. I like cats—"

"We do not cook cats here, Mrs Landry. The finest of lamb, beef, but no cats. How dare you insinuate this about our restaurant. These rumours can damage busi—"

"Rav, I'm not talking about food. I'm saying do you like cats?"

His brow furrowed. "Sometimes, Shelley, you are a strange lady. I am asking what you want to eat, and you are asking me if I like cats."

"Forget it," I said.

"Do I like cats? I'll write that down and take it to the chef who will kick my arse for not delivering your order to the kitchen in a timely manner because I'm discussing my love of pets."

"Hmmm, someone's becoming a grumpy little demon tonight, aren't they, Rav? We'll just take another few minutes to decide." I folded my arms across my chest.

"Uh." He stomped off.

"But we know what we want." Theo frowned.

"Yes, darling, but I'm going to annoy that little shit all night. I'm beginning to reconsider getting him a date."

After a few moments Rav returned to the table.

"So, my lovely lady and gent, could I now take your order?" It was killing him to be civil. This wasn't like Rav. I knew he was a demon, but I rarely actually saw it. I wondered what had caused the change.

"Yes, I'd like prawn puri, followed by lamb rogan josh, thank you. And a nice bottle of red wine for us to share."

"Nothing for me," said Theo.

"Are you not pretend eating?" Rav asked him.

"Actually, you can bring me a naan bread. Shelley will pretend she doesn't want any and then proceed to eat the whole thing."

I pulled a face at him.

"Thank you. I will be back shortly with your starter."

"Rav. Stop a minute. Why are you in such a bad mood?"

He huffed.

"Remember I talked about an irritating customer? Your adoptive parents called in earlier and I'm sorry, Shelley, but your father, he is an arsehole."

"Oh don't apologise, I already know this. What was he doing this time?"

"He asked for the hottest curry and then kept returning it saying it wasn't hot enough. If I could have, I would have flambeed his insides myself. I had to hold it in. I cannot be evil here. If I become evil here, then who knows what I could do to the lovely citizens of Withernsea? But that man, he drove me very close to the edge."

"Look, he's not here now. So just settle back. Is there a way to make the evil go away a bit?"

"Only if some happy things happen."

"Okay, how about if I tell you I'm going to try to set you up on a date?"

"Me?" Rav laughed. "Oh I am a lost cause, Shelley, don't waste your time."

"No, Rav, you are not. If we can get Theo a wife, we can get you one."

"Hey," Theo protested.

"Shelley, you married him yourself. That's like insulting your own choices. It makes me feel better though. You really think you might find me a date?"

"I promise to do my best, and I know about the whole getting past your mother thing and I'll bear that in mind."

"Ah, that's why you were asking me the question about pets. You were trying to fill in the application form again to update it. I will come into the agency some time. No need to ask me tonight. I prefer dogs, but cats are okay. Anyway, what brings you out tonight? Is it a special occasion?"

"We're trying to take Theo's mind off the fact his daughter is out on a date."

"Oooooh. Charlie is dating. And who is the lucky chap?" I noted that Rav didn't seem to be in any rush now to take our order in. It was going to be a long night at this rate.

"His name is Kai, and he is a merman. Obviously, he lives in Wyvern Sea."

"Niiicccee. And he is one of those with the big swishy tail and no legs. I wonder what his genitalia looks like?"

"Rav!"

"Sorry, thinking out loud. I shall go hand in the order. Bet you've wondered the same though, Shelley, yes?" Rav took one look at Theo's face and dashed off to take in our order.

"Theo, please count to ten because I can't explain away red eyes and fangs in here tonight, not even by blaming hot curry."

Theo shot up, grabbed the wine out of the other waiter's hand and drank some down straight from the bottle. "We'll need another bottle," he told him.

"Theo, you need to calm down. Kai assured you he

would take things slow when you threatened to drain him."

Rav brought over my starter. "Just a little something to nibble on. Save yourself for the exquisite main course."

Theo put his fist in his mouth.

"What's up with you now?" I said exasperated.

"Nibbling. Saving self for main course. I'm thinking of Kai with my daughter."

I placed my hands on my cheeks. This was so not turning out to be the relaxing meal I had envisaged. While Theo worked his way through another glassful of wine, I slowly ate and enjoyed my starter. I'd been tempted to make a joke with the word fishy in it and wished Kim were here. In fact, she'd have made the joke herself. I was missing my friend. I needed to go see her and the babies soon.

Rav brought the main course. "And here is the main course. Look how juicy that sauce is. Only the best. Jump right in, Shelley. Coat your tongue in all those divine flavours. Savour it. You'll wish you could just dive into it, be one with it. It is that amazing."

A pained noise came from Theo who now had blood running from his fist where he'd punctured through it with his fangs while his hand was in his mouth. I picked up the naan bread and threw it at him. "Get a grip, Theo," I yelled.

"For God's sake, I'm bleeding, and you are throwing foodstuffs at me... AGAIN," Theo yelled back.

I moved from my chair and licked his hand to close the wound. He was obviously too drunk to do it himself. "It's just wine," I reassured the other diners who were agog watching us. Then for good measure I picked up the naan bread and whacked Theo around the head with it again.

"Oh you two. You are such fantastic entertainment. You've cheered me right up," Rav said. "Enjoy the rest of your meal." And with that he left us.

"Rav! You need to help me drag Theo out to the cloakroom and then I can whizz us both home. He's drunk," I whispered as I paid the bill.

"I don't think I have ever seen my friend drunk before."

"Yes, well, your dear friend Theo didn't have a dating daughter before. He's not taking it so well."

"He is very lucky he has a daughter at all. I shall

remind him of this fact when he is sober, but for now, yes, I will help you."

Finally, ten minutes later, I managed to whizz us back to our bedroom where my drunk husband laid out across our bed. And then he started singing Kylie's *I can't get you out of my head*, but replaced 'you' with 'it'.

Our door flung open, and Charlie stood there in her pyjamas and robe. "What the hell is that noise? I was fast asleep." She stared at the bed and her jaw dropped. "My dad's singing?"

"That's debatable, but this is what you've done to him by growing up. He's got drunk and now he's singing. I thought it was the child who came home drunk while they were growing up, but your father's finding his own way through accepting your adulthood."

Theo opened his eyes, sat up, then whizzed in front of Charlie. "Daughter! You're back!" He sniffed the air around her. "Your virtue is intact. My baby. How I love you. You are Daddy's girl, do you know that?" He pinched her cheeks.

"Ow," Charlie screamed.

"Don't leave me, Charlie bear. Charlene left me. Now you will leave me."

"What's he on about, Mum?"

"That Kylie left *Neighbours*. You'll have to excuse me in a moment, Charlie, but needs must."

"Charlie warlie. I am so very proud of you. You are the queen. Not the princess like Kylie, Princess of Pop; but queen, like Madonna. Ooh, what Madonna do I know? Oh God, *Like a Virgin*."

"Out." I pressed my hands to Theo's temples and blue sparks flew. Theo hit the bed unconscious.

"I thought you couldn't use magic for your own needs?"

"Sometimes rules are made to be broken, Charlie. Rather I broke a rule than a vase over his head. Now, did you have a nice evening?"

"Mum, it was wonderful. Kai was the perfect gentleman and we got along really well."

"That makes me very happy. Now go get some sleep, or rather, go and replay the evening over and over in your mind."

"Oh, Mum, that's just what I was doing before I fell asleep. I can't help it. How did you know?"

I sighed. "Because I only just did it myself with your dad, and that is when I find this situation most weird. You're my daughter, you feel like my daughter, but I'm only twenty-seven myself."

"Well, we can be like those mother and daughters

that are more like sisters, can't we?" she said, kissing my cheek.

"I am very proud to be your mum, Charlie, no matter how strange. Never forget that."

"I won't. Love you, Mum. Love you, drunk Dad." She laughed and left the room.

I turned and stared at the passed out pale creature lying across the bed.

"What am I going to do with you?" I said, and I didn't mean about his position of slumber.

CHAPTER 11

SATAN

I was having far too much fun with this already. Debbie had proved quite the little mover in the bedroom. Seemed after she insisted on having a 'heart-to-heart' with me, that she had felt we were drifting apart. She thought it had taken her threatening me with divorce for me to see the error of my ways. What-ev-er. Her poor husband. I bet he was glad I'd taken over his body, stuffed him deep down inside himself where he ceased to exist. At least he didn't have to listen to her. If I got fed up with her talking, I'd taken to filling her mouth with something to shut her up. However, I'd just seen the buxom brunette at number twenty-two put her bins out in her sheer pyjamas, so Debbie might have to be dealt with another way soon.

According to my wife, the only thing they all knew

about the war was there would be one, and that it might involve a sausage roll. I'd never heard anything so stupid in my life, and believe me, when you'd been Satan you'd heard every excuse under the fiery, burning, excruciatingly painful rays of the sun while the new recruits tried their best to be freed from their new home in the bowels of hell.

This morning I had not been able to resist calling in at the coffee shop. I wanted to know if she could detect me, but no. As I thought, I only registered as Mark Linley at the moment while I still didn't have my powers. Now that was a problem I needed to sort out at my earliest convenience. I couldn't exactly get Withernsea back without having some kind of power. But then they'd talked about holding a wedding reception for my lovely and completely traitorous, backstabbing ex-assistant Lucy and the arseswipe she'd married. I'd killed him and then that bloody vampire had brought him back to life, well un-life. Hmmm, there'd be a wedding buffet. Maybe war could start with a sausage roll after all... especially if I poisoned them. I could rid myself of the do-gooding bastards in one fell swoop if I got the recipe right. It was food for thought. In the meantime, the dim-witted Samara had given me the perfect idea to distract them all.

Taking over the body of Mark Linley had been an

act of genius. Not surprisingly, no-one noticed he'd been taken over because he was a rancid slug of a man anyway. In fact, I'd done Hull and Withernsea a huge favour.

Tonight had been the icing on the cake. A tour of Wyvern Sea. Permission to go under the water and see what I could also command under there. I'd had to endure an hour with the extra do-gooding Polly and her new boyfriend, but it was all worth it for the information I had gathered.

Then I'd suggested Debbie and I go for an Indian where I'd had far too much fun tormenting my old colleague Rav. Yes, I was having a devil of a time. All I needed now was to secure the return of my evil powers. There must be a way and I would find it. It was quite a problem with my current plans for Withernsea domination that I didn't actually have any power. In the meantime, I would just have to concentrate on the fact I was wicked to the core.

I rang the Cupid Inc headquarters. "Oh hello there. One of your Cupids, Rebecca. She set me up with a beautiful woman who I'm pleased to say I have just proposed to. Could you give me a telephone number for her so I could thank her?"

A happy sing-song voice came down the line. I was almost sick on myself. "We can't give out personal information, but I can give you an email address for you to send your thanks. Now which Rebecca is it? Do you have her location?"

"Yes, Hornsea."

"Ah, do you have a pen and paper?"

"I do."

"Okay, that's rebeccawilkins, all one word." She spelled it out for me, "atcupidinc.com. That's inc for incorporated with a c, not ink like in a pen."

I hung up.

To: rebeccawilkins@cupidinc.com
From: yourfriend@gmail.com
Subject: Samara

Rebecca
I heard about your incident with Samara. Basically, she was in Jax's coffee shop in Withernsea telling everyone within listening distance about your unfortunate mishap down under (and we know I don't mean Australia, don't we?)
Here are my suggestions, as a secret supporter of everything you do in your role as Cupid representative for Hornsea.

1. Go to your bosses about Samara being helped by the dating agency.

2. Let anyone else know. Is there a company magazine?

3. Samara detests sausage rolls. Send her some to her grooming salon with a note that if she wants to bring it, you can too. (Anonymous of course, but she'll know who did it.)

4. Anything else you can think of to annoy her. She's far too loved up and happy and who wants that? (Yes for everyone else, but not for her, hey?).

From: someone else she picked on. Just because she's a pet groomer doesn't mean she can tell us how to shave our pussies, right?

I signed off. This should do the trick. Let the games begin. Samara had annoyed me by becoming loved up with that husband of hers, becoming the first couple of that damn dating agency, so she deserved what she got.

Now I just had to see what happened...

CHAPTER 12

SHELLEY

All was pretty quiet and peaceful for the next week. Charlie visited the sea each evening where Duke Brishon gave her lessons in sea politics and then she'd spend a few hours with Kai before returning home. I'd decided the best way to keep Theo from worrying was to keep him distracted. I was tired but in a good way.

Friday morning came, and yawning, I crossed the threshold of Jax's coffee shop to get a lovely hot brew. I think I needed an espresso chaser.

The door banged open and Samara hurtled through the door, her blonde curly locks bouncing all over the place, whipping me in the face as she finally stopped at my side.

"Shelley. Shelley. It's started. Ebony was right. It is to do with sausage rolls. Look!"

She plonked a tray full of fourteen freshly cooked sausage rolls on the counter. My stomach rumbled. Written in tomato sauce across them was:

THISISWARBITCH.

"I'm telling you, they're from that bitch Rebecca. I got a call from Cupid Inc HQ and I'm being full-on audited because she's told them I don't do anything; that I rely on the dating agency and fudge my figures. I'd only just got out of the last audit by getting Polly and Drake together."

I didn't tell her that actually I did that, because she had been instrumental in shooting her arrows into Keto to show the person Keto loved most was herself, which had paved the way for my sister and her boyfriend to get together for good.

"What are you going to do about it?"

"Me? We ask Charlie, don't we? Seeing as this is the war."

I took a drink of my coffee and closed my eyes to think this over. Surely this was not the war Charlie was prophesized to save us all from? But there was a declaration via sausage rolls, so I had to treat it as a possibility.

"I'm going to call the bitch." Before myself or Jax could stop her, her phone was out of her bag and she'd dialled a number.

"Hey, Bex. Thanks for the rolls. Oh stop pretending you don't know about them. Anyway, my friends are just sharing them. They said they're delicious, so I'm just checking you didn't put anything in them did you, or I'll have to phone the police? Just a warning are they? Well, I'm over here shitting my pants, babe. What's next, a Cornish pasty? You're very strange, do you know that?"

She laughed. "Is that right? Cupid's weekly magazine. I tell you what, whingebag mingebag. Why don't you come here and see if Shelley can set you up on a date? Because although I might be too lazy to get people together, at least I managed to get a guy myself and he didn't scream when he removed my panties because he thought a stray rabid dog was loose down there."

I could hear screaming at the other end of the phone.

"Bring it. Go to the magazine. See if I care." Samara hung up.

She looked from me to Jax and back again. "She's going to write an article for the weekly Cupid magazine, explaining how dating agencies are killing the Cupid business and making some of us lazy, and how something needs to be done to stop the global phenomenon of dating agencies. She thinks she can get enough people together to descend on Withernsea in a protest."

"Great. Protests against my dating agency. What amazing publicity that will be. How will I explain that away to the press?"

"They'll just think Cupid Inc is a rival dating agency. I just hope Cupid himself doesn't come down to earth and declare war on you. We don't want a war on love. That would be catastrophic."

"I'm sure Cupid will be happy to see love matches being made, however it's happening," I said.

"Well, maybe." She shrugged.

"What do you mean, maybe?"

"Cupid gets all the kudos for people falling in love, yeah? He's not going to be happy if the press get hold of the story and declare the Cupid system is outdated and agencies are the way forward. What if they say it's agencies all the way and Cupid is out?"

"Oh dear God. Do you mean to say that this

stupid Rebecca could cause Cupid himself to come to Withernsea and challenge me about my agency?"

"Yup."

"Okay, I'll speak to Charlie tonight. It would appear this could be the beginning of the war after all."

Chapter 13

Satan

I'd sat near the coffee shop bathroom with my back to the doorway while wearing a large black coat and hat. I'd made sure to sit across from a female customer who I made polite chitchat with which almost killed me, but it worked in not drawing attention to myself. The man had served me, so no one was the wiser that I was in the shop, or rather that Mark Linley was in the shop. I heard them discussing the results of my fiendish plan. It had come together perfectly.

And now, while they prepared to solve the oncoming war with Cupid they imagined was a possibility, I would accelerate my own plans for Withernsea domination.

First stop, to get my powers back.

I was the rightful Satan. Now to find the wrong one. The person who had taken my job.

The question was, how did a displaced Satan manage to scheme his job back? You'd have thought it would be difficult to hitch a lift to hell, and maybe for those less evil than myself it could be. I knew one thing; I was becoming increasingly frustrated with this middle-aged body I was inhabiting and was ready to change to a new model. With this aim in mind, I drove to Withernsea, parked up in the library car park, departed the very middle-aged-driver centric Honda Civic and made my way through the library entrance. Just as I had envisaged, the library was empty with the exception of the almost at retirement age librarian, and two youths who were throwing crisps at each other while sitting in front of the two outdated computers at the far end of the library. I wandered slowly around while I tried to work out the best place to leave Mark's body for a while. With any luck I wouldn't need to return to it at all. In the meantime, Mark would remain in an exhausted sleep mode for hours, so should anyone discover him—which was doubtful in the cemetery like library—they would be likely to just leave him be.

Either way, to be honest I didn't give a toss. If he did wake up and ramble about being possessed by the devil, then I'd be able to pick him up later from the local psychiatric hospital if I needed him.

The smell of damp, dogeared library books made my skin crawl. It was about time the libraries were burned down and everyone was given an e-reader. Maybe one of my first jobs back in Withernsea would be to torch the place. It would be the only way Withernsea would ever get a hot librarian that was for sure. Finally, after wandering around several bookshelves, I found a quiet corner with one chair next to the section on crossword puzzles and Sudoku. It was adjacent to the section on diet and exercise and likely to remain uninhabited for the rest of the day. I picked up a book about chess, sat in the chair and let the spark of energy that I currently was depart via Mark's mouth and started my journey out of the building towards Hanif's. It wasn't often I thanked the Lord—usually he was my enemy—but on this occasion I was grateful my exit was via Mark's mouth and not his backside given his middle-aged flatulence.

I knew from my time as Reuben, Theo's best friend, that Rav spent most of his spare time at the restaurant, mainly in order to escape his mother. He'd clean, prepare meals, and do maintenance, because no matter how hard the work was, it wasn't as hard work as his mother. I entered through a vent and moved through to the main restaurant area where Rav was wiping down tables and straightening menus. He was singing along to Kylie Minogue's, *Better the Devil You Know*. No doubt Theo had lent him the CD. If I'd have been able to, I would have laughed at the irony. Instead, I took over Rav's body. This time I had more of a fight on my hands given that Rav was a demon. He fought to try to expel me from his body, but given my past as Satan I was stronger. I pushed him down, so his thoughts and protests could no longer be heard and then I transported myself straight to Hell.

"Honey's, I'm home."

My replacement was nowhere to be seen. Instead, all around were bikini wearing young temptresses, all long hair and blow job mouths, with whips in their hands. Hell had become a cliché in my absence.

I walked up to one of the living blow-up dolls. "Where is the main guy, doll? I have an appointment with him."

She turned to me, looking me up and down. "He's

downstairs in the sauna. Would you like me to bleep him for you, Rav?"

"No, I'll find him, thank you."

"Okay. I didn't know you were on shift today. Do you fancy getting a drink later?"

Huh. I'd never scored a date in all the time I'd been here. Then again, I'd only employed the most troll-like looking people because then when they made goo-goo eyes at those stuck here, it added another layer to their punishments. Shelley reckoned she was awesome at running a dating agency, but I'd like to see her find the perfect date for Satan himself.

"Maybe later? Right now, I have some other hot stuff to deal with." That was if Rav survived my trip to Hell because once I encountered the current Satan, all bets were off.

"Okay, well hope to catch you later," Blow-up said with a taloned-nail wave.

I made my way down to the next level where the sauna was. Although the heat was punishment for anyone who ended up here through dreadful deeds, the staff here were employees and as such could make the most of the benefits of the heat. To that end, on this floor there were saunas, swimming pools, and steam rooms. We also had a hair salon that employees could use after they finished their shift so they could enjoy a conditioning treatment especially for heat damaged hair free of charge. See, I wasn't all bad. Actually, that was a total lie. I quite often replaced the contents of the conditioning treatment bottles with hair removal cream and blamed the intense heat for their hair falling out.

I didn't want to call the new guy Satan because as far as I was concerned he was an impostor and I was the real deal. Therefore, I decided to call him Bub, short for Beelzebub. I opened the door to the sauna and stepped inside.

"Hey, Dickwad." Okay, I'd changed my mind about his new name.

"Who is it?" Dickwad sat up from his reclined position on the lowest wooden bench and leaning forward scrunched up his eyes trying to make out who had entered the sauna. Was this guy for real? If anyone had dared to interrupt my break time in the sauna, I would have smitten them where they stood. Things had got too easy around here. Now I was back and things were going to change. You would have thought it would be a lot harder to take over the body of Satan —or as we called him now Dickwad—than just leaving the body of Rav and popping straight down the current Satan's throat. But sure enough that's all I had to do, because my successor had been so confident that he was evil incarnate that he'd failed to assume there could be anyone else more evil in his domain. He should have been right, for there was no one eviller than Satan—except of course for another Satan. My atoms and molecules fought his valiantly. If you'd ever had terrible acid reflux you would have a clue of what it would have felt like. Imagine you'd consumed curry, whiskey, chocolate, coffee, and lemon juice and then gone straight to bed to lie down and you'd have some idea of the pain of our fight for supremacy. Of course I won, completely shutting down any aspect of Dick-wad. His body was in its mid-30s, fit and toned, and a welcome change from Mark Linley's. Now I just needed to work out what to do with Rav. He currently lay exhausted on the floor of the sauna. I debated putting him in there, jamming the door from the outside and dealing with him later. Then I remembered the offer he'd just received from Miss blow-up doll. Picking him up and lying him on one of the loungers outside the sauna, I returned to the level above and found the woman again. Of course this time she was faced with Satan, her boss, not Rav. She straightened up, fear widening her eyes. I'd forgotten how good it felt to have people completely terrified to be in my presence and I felt myself getting hard. Luckily Dickwad liked tighty-whiteys which held my dick down my trouser leg and didn't advertise to anyone that I could knock someone the fuck out with the contents of my briefs.

"Sir, can I be of assistance?" she asked, clearly hoping I said no.

"Actually, you can," I replied. She looked so nauseous that I wondered what Dickwad had been making her do while he was here. "Rav is downstairs on a lounger. He wasn't due to work today and came into the sauna spouting some nonsense about having been possessed, and then collapsed. He appears to be extremely exhausted. Could you keep him company until he wakes and then offer him a massage, drink, and anything else he desires until he feels better? Please insist, and reassure him that when he arrived, he had a temperature and was delusional. Suggest that he relaxes fully before returning home."

"Yes, sir." Blow-up doll looked highly relieved. "I will get on that straight away."

With any luck that's exactly what she would do, see an opportunity and get on Rav without delay. Unless things had changed significantly, Rav wasn't used to many offers from the opposite sex, or any sex for that matter, and would quickly accept the explanation given by the beautiful woman in front of him who was offering him his every desire.

"Sorry, I can't recall your name?" I asked blow-up.

"Frida, sir."

"Ah yes, that's right," I lied as if I'd known it. "Frida. Look after Rav in any way he needs, take him for a drink if you like. Take the rest of your shift off. In fact, if Rav needs it, you can both have the entire weekend off, okay? Just make sure you keep him in your sights until he seems to have fully recovered."

"I'll see if he wants to come and stay at my apartment," she said, her face lighting up.

"What a splendid idea, Frida. Insist on it," I told her. That would give me time to create hell before Rav could potentially give his stupid friends a clue I was back. Frida left and I smiled widely, looking around at the familiar environment. I was back in Hell. My staff were my playthings. I was the puppet master who held all the strings and I intended to dangle them until they strangled Shelley and her pathetic family and friends.

It was good to be me. I now ruled Hell once more and it wouldn't be long before I ruled Withernsea again too.

CHAPTER 14

SHELLEY

When I got home from work, I found my daughter asleep on the sofa. I wasn't sure if she was tired from her constant travelling to under the sea, or if she was bored and falling asleep because reruns of Jeremy Kyle were no longer of interest.

I nudged her gently so as not to startle her, knowing from experience that you didn't make a supernatural jump unless you wanted things to end badly. Strange groaning noises came from my daughter's mouth while her eyes opened and she oriented herself with her surroundings.

"Hey, Mum. Is it teatime already?"

"Not quite, hun. I finished early and left Lucy to it. There's something we need to discuss. The war might have started."

This made my daughter wake up quickly. She shot up, sitting against the headboard. "What do you mean the war might have started? What happened? Has someone threatened you?"

I perched on the side of her bed. "No, not me. It's Samara. She got in a falling out with another Cupid representative. Today they sent her fourteen sausage rolls. Each one had a letter on it and the letters spelled 'this is war bitch'. Apparently, this woman is going to write an article for a magazine and assemble a protest march against dating agencies. Mine in particular, as she thinks Samara is benefiting unfairly from it."

"Hmm, it certainly has the sausage roll component, but Ebony also mentioned heat, so maybe this is nothing."

"They fell out in a spa. They'd just come out of the sauna when Samara decided to draw attention to the fact that the woman hadn't shaved her private area correctly."

"God, she didn't?"

"It's Samara. Of course she did. Anyway, it would appear that this rivalry has been building for some time and that this brought things to a head."

"But how does this lead to a war? Even if people protest against the dating agency, surely it's just a storm in a teacup?"

"Not if enough Cupid representatives take offence at dating agencies. If Rebecca gets enough support behind her and Cupid representatives begin to feel threatened that their jobs are on the line, then potentially someone could try to cause us harm, try to take us out of the equation. It wouldn't be the first time the dating agency has been attacked, although funnily enough I employed the woman who damaged it last time. Maybe I just need to offer this Rebecca a different job?"

"It's just not what I was expecting from a prophecy about war. I thought it would be interspecies fighting, humans versus supernatural, and me being a combination of Wonder Woman, Jessica Jones, and the woman from the Matrix films. I imagined I'd have to become close to death before rising in one last final attempt at destroying the main villain and then everyone rushing to my side congratulating me on my feats of strength and endurance."

"Charlie, this is not a Marvel or DC film. I'm going to stop the Netflix subscription if you're not careful. Let me guess you are already picturing Kai playing Aquaman in this vision of yours?"

Charlie gave me a guilty shifty look.

"I know what you mean though. I myself thought there would be much more to the main battle of Withernsea than a fight amongst Cupid reps. However, everything Ebony said she saw in her visions has come true."

"Perhaps I should ring Ebony and get her opinion on what is happening with the Cupid reps? In the meantime, I guess I should make the first steps towards calming this woman down and stopping potential war."

I handed my daughter a piece of paper containing Rebecca's details. "If you need any more information, don't forget your father is an expert at intel."

"Yes, I bet there's a full report upstairs on a certain Kai Oceanson." She raised a brow.

"How's everything going anyway? Are you two getting on well?"

My daughter's face lit up. She was most definitely falling in love. "He's amazing. Kind, funny, and a rival for any superhero any day of the week."

"Oh, Charlie, I am so happy for you. I was worried in case he turned out to not be who you felt he was."

"I know it's strange, Mum, that I knew he was the one even when I was in baby form. But it's just like something chemical within us responds to the other. It's a bit like Twilight with the imprinting."

"Yes, and I thought that was really weird when I

watched the film. Didn't think I'd have my own fast-growing child."

"What do you think my own children will be like, Mum? If I am made up of all of the different species, how on earth am I supposed to know what my babies will be like? I mean will I have hybrids? Maybe they'll have a dragon head and a werewolf body."

I could see Charlie was on the verge of hysteria. "Whatever your children look like, you will love them anyway, Charlie. But I'm glad you've raised the subject. I don't want to pry in your, let's call them 'private shenanigans', but how far have things moved along? I know you know the facts of life and where the clinic is to get contraception, but if you need me to explain things to you in greater detail, I am here for you."

"Ew, Mum. Change the subject immediately. We're not at that stage yet, and when we get to it, neither you nor Dad will know anything about it."

I laughed at the expression on her face. "Okay, I'll not mention it again. But you must understand, I had to raise the subject because I'm a mum and that's what we do."

It was then we heard an immense amount of groaning coming from my bedroom. "I think your dad might be awake, and experiencing the morning after the night before, or in his case the twilight after the night before."

"Oh, Mum. Please say we can go and torment Dad. Please, please, please."

Well of course I wasn't going to refuse my daughter when we could have heaps of fun in the process. We made our way upstairs, being as loud as possible. I walked into our bedroom and threw myself down on the bed at the side of my husband.

"Theo, Theo, are you awake? We have an emergency. Charlie is pregnant and the babies are growing at an accelerated rate. We reckon we have about thirty minutes before she starts to deliver."

Theo leaped out of bed so fast that he hit the ceiling, the wall, then bounced on the floor, before leaping up and yelling "Whaaaaaaaaaaattt? I'll kill him. Where is he? I'm going to kill the bastard. How dare he? Did I not make it clear enough to him that I would drain his blood drop by drop, making him a merman pincushion or an extremely slow dripping shower head? That his body would get weaker and weaker, and that I would find parasitic demons to feast on every slow drop causing him the worst pain he could ever imagine."

My normally pale-faced vampire husband was

currently puce. His eyes were ruby red, his fangs descended, and his sentences punctuated by hissing.

"Joking," I said loudly in a singsong voice.

Theo stood stock still and he turned his head towards me in infinitesimally small moves. The hairs on the back of my neck rose because his movements and the look on his face chilled me to the bone. I had never seen my husband look like the vampire predator he was before. He'd always been the gentleman vampire, polite at every turn. I wondered what I'd done. As I turned to look at Charlie, I saw she'd stilled and was no longer finding the situation amusing. She looked at me, eyes wide.

Theo made a hissing sound that made me and Charlie scream and dive under the covers at the same time. I don't know what we thought the bedcovers were going to offer in terms of protection, but that's what instinct made us do. Theo had taken me so much by surprise that it was like my powers had frozen. Anyway, how could I hurt the one I loved when I had caused this situation in the first place?

I peeked my head out from under the covers. He was standing at the end of the bed, his fangs bared. "Theo, darling. I'm so sorry. We thought it would be funny with you having a hangover. I realise now it was ill judged. I can promise you that Charlie is not even having sex, never mind pregnant. Look, she's here at the side of me. Charlie, lift up your t-shirt and show your dad there is no bump."

Theo began to move towards us with the same agonisingly slow, predatory movements. We backed up against the headboard. What was I going to do? I needed to get my husband back fast. He flew above us so that he hovered just inches above where we laid. His body faced down and his face took on the evilest grimace I had ever seen. Then his face relaxed, and he burst out laughing.

"Joking!"

"Excuse my language, Charlie, but, Theo, you utter fucking bastard. I almost crapped my pants. I genuinely thought I'd turned you into an evil vampire and was just debating whether if it came to the crunch, I could kill you in order to save myself and our daughter. It's a good job you didn't take this much further, or we might have found out the answer and you could be a pile of dust right now."

But I'm not sure he heard me, for he had dropped to the floor at the side of the bed where he currently lay in a heap of giggles while he clutched his stomach. I turned to Charlie, "I think we can safely say your dad's hangover has worn off and that our wind-up went spectacularly wrong. I think we'll just concentrate on saving Withernsea from war."

Theo stopped laughing, sat up, and stared in our direction, his expression turning serious. "Let this be a lesson to you. That while you both have supernatural powers, you are dealing with other species of paranormal beings and some are more evil than you could ever imagine. Don't underestimate anybody, either supernatural or human."

Huh. Not only had we not had any fun, we had also had our arses handed back to us by Theo. I didn't know about my daughter, but I knew I now felt rather stupid and completely ill-prepared for a future war.

"I think this weekend, Charlie, it might be worth you getting in touch with Frankie and having some lessons in all of the supernatural species, learning their strengths and weaknesses. Because while we think the war might be centred around the current situation with the Cupids, as your father says, right now we can't underestimate anybody. Because what if we are wrong? Talk to Ebony, contact Rebecca, and go to see Frankie. Then if you have spare time by all means go to see Kai. But right now, your priorities have to be with training yourself so you are the most badass queen Withernsea has ever seen, armed with as much information as you can be. I think you also need to arrange sessions with the leaders of each species to learn their combat. I'm sure Alyssa will help you with Were skills. You need to do all this as soon as possible, Charlie."

"Well, Mum, to say we came upstairs to have a laugh at Dad's expense, I appear to have lost my whole sense of humour right now."

I knew how she felt. We had come to torment a hungover vampire, but we had ended up with the sobering lesson.

CHAPTER 15

CHARLIE

That hadn't gone exactly to plan, had it? And now my weekend was set to be busier than ever. But there was one thing for sure. If war was coming, and my life was going to be on the line, there was no way I was dying a virgin. So I would contact Ebony, I would get in touch with Rebecca, and I would train and learn about everything supernatural; but, on Sunday evening I would be under the sea seducing a certain merman and nothing was going to stop me.

Without further ado it was time to tackle my immense to-do list starting with contacting Ebony. My mobile phone rang, and I took it out of my pocket seeing from the screen that it was the lady herself. It was really annoying when she did that.

"Hey, Ebony, so I guess you already know what

I'm going to phone you about seeing as you've rung me first."

"Yes, I just experienced a vision of you calling; only Henry and I have plans. Therefore, I have phoned you first, so that I may return to my husband at my earliest convenience."

"I'm very sorry that I might want to see whether or not we are at war and that it might interfere with what obviously is you getting down and dirty with your husband."

"Darling, I'm a seer. I have also had the most unwelcome vision of how your Sunday evening works out, so don't talk to me about prioritising my love life when you just want to clear the decks so you can get to yours."

"Ew, seriously, your visions extend to seeing our private lives? That is gross."

"After a while, you get used to seeing your friends naked flesh. I only got the vision because it must in some way be connected with something important."

"But let me guess, you have no idea what that is?" Ebony's visions were nearly always like this, just pieces and fragments with no real explanation or warning of what they represented.

"Don't get snippy with me, just because I know what happens on Sunday evening and you don't,"

Ebony said with a hint of superiority, satisfaction, and smugness in her tone.

"Does it all go okay, Ebony?" My nervousness was recognisable by the tremble that appeared in my voice.

"You'll be fine, darling. Once I began to get the vision, I quickly turned it off, so I don't actually know everything that happens. I didn't want it putting me off my own date with my husband."

God help me. "Ebony, the reason I am ringing you, or, well, you have called me—if it wasn't clear in your vision—is that there have been developments with the war in Withernsea. Apparently, Samara has created a situation with another Cupid rep called Rebecca, to the extent that now Rebecca has sent a threat to Samara via a freshly cooked batch of sausage rolls which spelled-out the threat 'this is war bitch'. Now, this Rebecca is threatening to bring a protest to the doors of Mum's dating agency and to potentially bring down the wrath of Cupid himself. Rebecca is going to the Cupid magazine where she will highlight what she perceives to be the devastation wrought by dating agencies to Cupid Inc. What are your feelings about this? Does it fit with your visions of the war? It all started after a visit to a spa where Rebecca had been in the sauna, so the heat aspect is covered."

There was a pause from the other end. "Though it

does fit with the things I said, I don't feel this is the war. The feelings of heat I get are intense, as if I am burning from the inside out. There's also an overwhelming sense of evil now when I think about it."

I didn't say that she could have done with mentioning that before. "Okay, Ebony. I'll give this Rebecca a call and arrange to meet her. Then I can find out what she's about and what her plans are once and for all, and see whether she is inherently evil, or just embarrassed that her hairy vagina was on display to all her colleagues at the spa."

"I find it hard to have sympathy for her. We all know it is important to give our appearance the utmost attention. One can never know when our bodies may end up on display, be that a chance encounter with a gorgeous man; or slipping on a banana skin, while wearing a tutu while having gone commando. By the way, I made the second situation up, but it could happen. Can you imagine if that had happened to Sarah Jessica Parker in the beginning of Sex and the City? The ad on the bus would probably have ended up being sponsored by Veet."

"Actually, come to think of it, there was a similar scene to all this in the second Sex and the City film where Miranda hadn't shaved."

"You mean someone actually did watch that film

after all?" Ebony said. "Did you not see the reviews? There was a reason there was no third film and I'm sure hairy vaginas were the real reason. No one wants to see that, ever."

Dear God. I had forgotten what conversations with Ebony about looking your best at all times were like. My mum said she could barely walk past the shop without Ebony dragging her in and doing something like threading her eyebrows before letting her go to the office for the day.

"Right, well thank you, Ebony. I must get going and arrange to see this Rebecca. I will leave you to return to that husband of yours. Have a good evening."

"Oh, honey, I intend to." She ended the call.

I thought about what Ebony said, and checking the time I saw it was getting late. I decided I needed to get something to eat, something to drink (probably an O-neg), and then before I did anything else, I was going to get in the shower, shave my legs and underarms, pluck my eyebrows, and apply fake tan. Because whatever I did next, I would do it looking amazing. I did not want to go down in history remembered as being the Hairy Queen of Withernsea.

On Saturday morning, I went downstairs and fixed myself a coffee, then returned to bed and stayed under the duvet for an hour while talking to Kai. He understood that I wouldn't be able to see him until Sunday evening. Once I'd ended my conversation with Kai, I picked up the piece of paper with Rebecca's details and phoned the number written there. It rang out a few times before she answered.

"Hello."

"Hello, is that Rebecca?"

"Yes, my name is Rebecca. Who is this?"

Here went nothing. Once I explained who I was, I fully anticipated Rebecca would hang up.

"My name is Charlie. I'm the daughter of Shelley Landry. Please don't hang up. I want to talk to you about Samara."

"If you're a friend of Samara's, then I doubt I have anything to say to you, or anything that you could say to me. She's embarrassed me so much I can barely show my face around Hornsea."

I decided the best way to try to get through to Rebecca was to give her my time and attention and listen to her perceived plight. "Oh I can imagine. Samara has always been a bit foot in mouth. She acts first and then realises what she's done later. I honestly don't think she will have meant any malice at that point. However, I wasn't there and so I don't feel like I can defend her. The reason I've called is that obviously my mum runs Withernsea Dating Agency and she is concerned that there could be trouble from Cupid reps and the public brought to her door because of Samara's behaviour."

"The thing is, that although Samara is a complete bitch and I do believe she did do it on purpose because she always wants to be the centre of attention, the fact remains that cupiding is becoming more and more difficult due to the increase in dating agencies, both in towns and cities, and online. We have monthly quotas and it gets increasingly impossible to meet our targets when everyone is competing for the same pool of single people. I used to matchmake a lot of supernaturals before your mum's agency opened as there wasn't really anywhere else for them to go. It was a way that I managed to meet my numbers. Since she opened the supernatural division of her agency it has made my own job harder."

"I totally get you, babe, but that's the thing with business, it's always evolving. How long has Cupid been doing this biz for now? It sounds like maybe Cupid Inc needs an overhaul. Not to audit Samara, but to have a look at its internal structure and see if there's a way that Cupid Inc can run alongside dating agencies or do something that a dating agency can't do."

"Like what?" Rebecca asked.

"Well, just off the top of my head for instance, my mum doesn't have time to look in great detail about why someone is not successful at dating. She can use her computer systems, but what about the completely undateable? You could spend time with that person one-on-one, look to see if they have any obvious problems or flaws, and work with them to either change, or find a person who loves them warts and all."

"You might have an idea there, you know? Can you do me a favour? Don't mention this to Samara. If you tell her, she will take it straight to Cupid himself, make out it's all her idea, and then it can be Samara the Superstar all over again."

"She is really nice underneath her brash exterior, you know. It's just while the outside package is pretty it still manages to hurtle around like a baby elephant. But I won't say anything. You take this idea to Cupid if you want to and see what he says. Funnily enough, my mum said she might end up offering you a job. Maybe instead you can still work for Cupid Inc alongside my mum's and other dating agencies, finding love for the people the dating agencies can't find matches for?"

"We'll have to agree to disagree about Samara,

because I can't forgive her for what she did. It's not my fault I'd broken my glasses the day before. Well, it kind of is, because I'd sat on them. It was just unfortunate that when I came out of the sauna my swimsuit had moved to the side just slightly. No one would have noticed if Samara hadn't drawn their attention to it. It wasn't like there was a gorilla situation down there. It didn't look like Tom Selleck's chest hair. The worst thing was the gossip got back to my team in Hornsea and since then my colleague, Felix, hasn't been able to look me in the eye. I was sure he was about to ask me out before this. So not only has Samara made me a laughingstock across the regional division, it's also made me an embarrassment in my own team and potentially cost me a date."

It sounded to me that all Rebecca had needed was someone to listen to her. "Rebecca, it sounds to me like you have the perfect guinea pig to practice on. Because you, according to what you said are currently an undateable. All you have to do is pretend you are one of your clients, start from there, and bag yourself a date with Felix. So, what do you think, Bex? A date, and a chance to impress Cupid himself, leading to a potential new side to the business." I prayed I'd done enough to settle the situation.

"Charlie, you've turned out to be like my

guardian angel, or something. Before you rang, I'll be honest, I was full of rage, and trying to work out how I could get revenge on Samara. With all the stress of trying to reach my targets, alongside my recent humiliation, all I could think about was going to the Cupid Inc magazine and causing a stir in Withernsea on Samara's turf. But your call has helped me see another way forward, one where I can get some Cupid kudos, a potential romance, a new career, and get my reputation back on track. Onwards and upwards."

Wow! This had gone better than I could ever have expected. If this was indeed the war of Withernsea, then I reckoned I'd just prevented it. That would mean I didn't have to learn approximately seventeen different kinds of species fighting and could go to see Kai straightaway.

"About Samara. Is it possible that for now you could ignore her? Just until I get the chance to have a chat with her and try to point out to her how what she did was insensitive. I'm sure she will apologise profusely when she realises just how much she has upset you."

"Yes, sure, that's fine. To be honest, if things with Cupid go well, then I won't care what Samara is doing anyway. However, an apology in future would be appreciated. In the meantime, I'll ignore her, as long as she ignores me and leaves me the hell alone."

"No more deliveries of threatening sausage rolls, okay?"

"Fine. She didn't seem too bothered about them anyway, despite the fact I'd been told she hated sausage rolls."

WTF?

"What do you mean you'd been told she hated sausage rolls?"

"Well, the anonymous email I received about Samara from my secret supporter said so. It said for me to tell my managers at Cupid Inc about her behaviour, to go to the magazine, and to send some sausage rolls to the grooming salon because she absolutely hated them."

For a few moments I didn't say a word in reply because my mind was trying to process the fact that Rebecca had been set up. In fact, we all had. Whoever had sent Rebecca the email had deliberately tried to divert attention away from their own plan. Basically, whoever had sent the email was the person planning on starting the war.

My heart plummeted. I'd still need to train, and now I needed to try to find out who had sent Rebecca the email. We had to be on our guard at all times because the person behind it was playing a clever game with us all.

"Are you still there?" Rebecca asked.

"Yeah, I am. Listen, I might need to ask you a favour in return. I know it's the first time you've ever heard from me, and I don't know how much you know about the politics of Withernsea, but I am prophesised to save Withernsea from a great war."

"Sorry, in Hornsea we don't tend to hear much about other areas. It's only the fact that Samara seems to love trying to get attention despite the fact she is the worst Cupid rep in the whole country, that I've had anything to do with Withernsea. That sounds really bad, Charlie. What favour is it that you need? I don't mind as long as I don't have to go into battle. I've had enough of that lately with Samara."

"I just need to try to find out who sent you the email. I wonder if there's any way you could contact your network, anyone really, see if you can find anything out. I know it's probably like looking for a needle in a haystack, but it's worth a try because I believe the person who sent this message to you is the one trying to cause trouble in Withernsea. By sending you the email, it led me to believe that the prophesy involved the Cupid reps and now I see this is doubtful."

"Oh, Charlie, yes. There is no way we would be at the centre, or at the start for that matter of any war. No matter our bickering internally, we are all about love. I will do what I can to find out where the message may have come from and I'll let you know. Thanks once again for calling me today. You have been an amazing help and I now feel positive about the future. It seems to me that you are a special, amazing person, and I can understand why you were chosen to save Withernsea."

Oh my. I had dreaded making this call, expecting to have to deal with a complete bitch, and I'd actually encountered a really lovely person. Now she'd put everything in context and reminded me what Cupid reps were all about, it did seem stupid to have thought they might have started the Withernsea war. We said our goodbyes, and I went downstairs and updated my mother on the contents and outcome of my conversation with Rebecca.

"It's great there won't be any protests outside the dating agency," Mum said. "However, it means we are no nearer to finding out who is behind the war."

"True, but it does prove that the person or persons responsible are already setting forth their mission to unleash war or evil upon Withernsea. The message sent to Rebecca was done with malice and to cause friction in the community. They were obviously intent on causing trouble or to divert our attention away from their own dastardly plans. Mum, we really do need to be extra vigilant. To be looking for anyone acting strangely, and to keep an eye on any newcomers to Withernsea. Particularly anyone who might suddenly join the dating agency to get close to us."

"I'll make sure your father does deep research on any new application from either human or supernatural before they are taken onto our books."

I thanked my mum, grabbed some lunch, and then headed to Alyssa's where she was going to give me my first combat training of the day.

***

When I returned home on Saturday evening, I felt battered and bruised. After seeing Alyssa, I'd visited Tristan, then gone through to Frankie's for some further teaching on supernatural species' strengths and weaknesses. I didn't know which was harder: combat, or trying to keep up with Lucy's sarcasm. To say she was no longer a demon and had been given a job as an earth angel, she was still a force to be reckoned with. I returned with a list of dos and don'ts for Friday's wedding reception, including that if the DJ played a single bar of *Gangnam Style*, she would light a match under Jax's sprinklers. I didn't bother explaining that the music was coming from my iPod attached to a speaker because it was the cafe, not a nightclub, but I quickly deleted *Gangnam Style* from the wedding playlist, along with *Celebration*, *Saturday Night*, and *The Birdie Song*.

A large part of Sunday daytime was spent in bed because my muscles screamed every time I tried to move myself. I'd thought having such a mix of supernatural ability, I'd get away with aches and pains, but I guess like with anything you had to use it or lose it. After a nice long soak in the tub, I went downstairs where I consumed double my usual amount of O-neg. I felt it run along my system, repairing torn muscles and easing the ache in my joints. A future lesson had been learned, double the blood before and after combat training.

Tomorrow, I would be back seeing different supernaturals for more training, and seeing Frankie again for more lessons on my peers, or should that be subjects? It still seemed very strange to comprehend that I was the Queen of both Withernsea and Wyvern Sea. But now it was time to forget the woes of Withernsea and go underwater to see my man.

I don't know which made me more nervous.

CHAPTER 16

CHARLIE

Daniel once more brought me to the door of Kai's cottage. Kai opened the door, a beaming smile across his face. The same smile was no doubt mirrored on my own face. My cheeks were aching with it. It had only been a couple of days since we had last seen each other, but it had felt like a lifetime.

Kai directed me straight through his living room, through his kitchen, and out of the rear door, onto the patio where we walked towards his workshop. Just inside the outbuilding I could see a large shape wrapped in a sheet, with a large ribbon around it tied in a bow.

"I missed you, but it gave me a chance to finish your gift." Kai grabbed my hand and pulled me towards the gift.

"Wow, Kai, I was expecting you to have a big package, but this is really something." I winked and watched as my beautiful man blushed. I had obviously spent too much time in Kim's presence and wanted to bite out my own tongue.

I stood in front of the gift and turned to him. "Can I open it now?"

"Yes, of course."

I reached to the bow at the back and unwrapped the ribbon. Then I removed the sheet. Below, I found the most exquisitely carved chair. Made of driftwood, it had a smooth seat and back but gnarled legs. It was a sheer thing of beauty, and a testament of his talent at his craft.

"Oh, Kai, it is stunning."

"Not as stunning as the woman I made it for," he told me. "I know you wear no airs and graces, but I believe that my queen needs a throne. Therefore, I have made you this chair that you can either keep here or have transported back to the farmhouse. You can use it as a dressing table chair or a desk chair, whatever you want, but I want you to know that as far as I'm concerned this is the throne for my queen." He moved closer to me, taking me in his arms, and staring down into my eyes. "Charlie, I love you."

My knees went weak, and I had to sit on the chair.

"Is this why you made it? Did you know you were going to make my legs turn to jelly and I'd need somewhere to rest?" I looked back at him, "Kai, I love you too."

Kai moved towards me, lowered himself onto his knees, leaned forward and crashed his mouth to mine. We became a tangle of lips, and teeth, and tongues, until after a few minutes Kai broke our kiss and moved back.

"My apologies, Charlie, for getting carried away. I wish to respect you, but you have to appreciate, it's hard for me to resist."

"Yeah, I can see that," I joked as my gaze fixed upon his groin area. Kai blushed again and I found it so endearing that he was a little shy around me when I was the virgin. I knew Kai had not had many lovers and this made me happy, because I might be the queen of Wyvern Sea but I was still insanely jealous of anyone who had been with my man. Standing up from my seat, I grabbed hold of Kai's hand and led him back across the patio, through the kitchen, and into the living room, where I paused at the bottom of the stairs. My heart thudded so hard in my chest, I didn't know how Kai couldn't hear it and how the walls weren't shaking with the ricochet from it. This was the moment I had been waiting for. I turned back to Kai, swallowing before I uttered a word, my mouth was so dry.

"Kai, I also have a gift for you. My gift is to be given to you in your bedroom. Therefore, I need to lead you upstairs in order to give it to you."

I could see he was about to protest, to say he was prepared to wait, like the gentleman I knew he was.

"Kai, I don't want you to be gentle with me. I want you to make love to me and hold nothing back. I fear the war is coming and I don't want to regret not having lived my life fully. I belong to you. My heart belongs to you. My soul belongs to you. Now please, don't make me beg, well, not at first anyway. Take me to bed, Kai."

He nodded. And he didn't need any further encouragement. He picked me up, put me over his shoulder and ran with me up the stairs. Placing me down outside his bedroom door, he opened the door, put on his bedside light to create ambience, and moved over to his docking station where he put on some soft background music. Then he walked back over to me, lifted me off my feet and slowly walked with me towards the bed where he placed me down with reverence.

Kai removed my clothes oh-so-slowly, kissing, nibbling, and trailing his tongue over every revealed inch of my skin. I was a puddle of goo. My nerves had completely disappeared. It all felt so right. I opened my eyes and watched as Kai removed his leggings, and what he revealed did not disappoint. He joined me in bed and returned to kissing every single inch of my body. His fingers dipped down low where he played me like a musical instrument. He was the musician, and he showed me he knew how to play well. Before long, I erupted around his fingers, my entire body shaking as I came down.

"Are you okay?" he checked with me.

"I am more than okay, Kai," I reassured him before leaning forward and pulling his face back towards mine where I kissed him within an inch of his life. There was more kissing, licking, nibbling, touching, and then I felt Kai's hard length as he positioned himself against my entrance. Once more he checked that I was okay and ready. I was more than ready. I knew that at first it could be uncomfortable and hurt, and sure enough at first his thrusts felt like small burns as he entered me. Kai remained gentle, until I reassured him that I was okay and then his arousal took over and he began to increase his pace. Pleasure burst through the pain of before and I met his thrusts, raising my hips trying to get him deeper inside me.

"Oh, Kai. Don't stop, don't stop," I screamed.

He increased his thrusts further and placed a finger on my clit. That was it. I became a bomb of lust and then I detonated, climaxing hard around his cock. With a groan, Kai came inside me.

We collapsed back against his sheets, and Kai pulled me into his arms, pulling the duvet cover over us. "How was that for you?" he asked. "You're not too sore, are you?"

"No. I'm a little sore, but Kai, it was everything I had hoped for. I feel even closer to you now."

We fell asleep in each other's arms and when I woke Monday morning, I realised I wasn't that sore after all. So we did it all over again, three times!

It was after I managed to extract myself from my cloud of lust, that I realised I'd not gone home, or even called or messaged home to let them know I was staying over.

Oh my god, my dad...

CHAPTER 17

SHELLEY

I t was a given to hate Mondays, but this Monday really was the pits. So my body could exist with the barest of sleep, but being kept up all night by my husband, and not in a good way, meant I felt like death warmed up.

Theo had spent the entire night and all the hours of dawn pacing the house and asking me how he could get permission to go under the sea to drag his daughter back home. It had taken me hours upon hours to get Theo to realise that his now grown-up daughter could do what she wanted. However, I did agree with him that we were presuming she had stayed out with Kai, and a text from her would have been appreciated to stop her father from alternately going between apoplexy at Kai taking her innocence and worry that the queen had been abducted and wondering when we were going to receive a ransom note.

I sent Charlie a text asking her to just let us know she was okay when she received the message. I was about to leave the house to go to the office when I received a return text.

Charlie: I am so sorry. I fell asleep at Kai's. I didn't mean to worry anyone, but I appreciate I will have done. Back soon. Just want to check first if Dad is all menacing vampire and threatening to kill Kai.

I texted her back.

Mum: Your dad was a mess... Try to remember to send us a quick text in future. I know you're grown up now, but we'd worry anyway, impending war or not. Hope you had a lovely evening. I'm off to work now xo

She sent another.

Charlie: Best evening ever! Kai has crafted me the most beautiful chair. I'm going to bring it home with me. He says it's my throne lol!

I had a feeling that my daughter was beyond happy from sitting on something, but that it wasn't the chair. However, I wouldn't share my musings with her father.

Theo returned to the kitchen after yet another perimeter check. "Have you heard from her yet?"

"Yes, she just texted. She apologised but said she fell asleep at Kai's. She is on her way back now. Apparently, he has made her a chair, and she's bringing it back with her."

Theo let out a deep exhale, something I always found amusing bearing in mind we didn't breathe. "Oh, this is good, she fell asleep. Hopefully, Kai covered her with nice warm blankets and looked after her. I can't wait to see the chair. It seems Kai is very talented with those hands of his."

I placed my hand over my mouth, and made sure my mind was shuttered off, so that Theo couldn't detect my amusement. I didn't know whether my husband was really being stupid or had just decided to live in a land called denial. Either way, he had calmed down, and I had no intention of setting him off again.

Theo excused himself and finally went off to bed. I headed to the hallway where I shoved my feet into my shoes, grabbed my bag, put on my coat, and whizzed off to work.

No sooner was I sat behind my desk than my phone rang. I answered the call from my adoptive mother before having to hold the phone away from my ear as she screamed down it hysterically.

"Calm down. I have no idea what you are saying. Take a deep breath; what is the matter?" Then I listened as she informed me that she had been at the hospital all weekend after Mark had been found unconscious at the back of the library.

"I don't even know what he was doing there, Shelley. He was certainly not doing the puzzles. That in itself is a puzzle. He never does puzzles. He refuses point blank to watch Countdown in an afternoon if he's on a day off. I don't understand why he was there. So far they have diagnosed he is suffering from complete exhaustion, but he's yet to say a word. But it's his eyes, Shelley, they just seem filled with fear. Do you think I have worn him out with too much sex and now he's scared of me?"

Of all the things I expected her to say, that had not been one of them, and it'd filled me with a mental image far scarier than anything I had envisaged thinking of war in Withernsea.

"I'm sure that's not it. Maybe he hadn't been feeling very well and so had gone into the library to rest and the only seat free had been near the puzzles? Did the librarian say anything?"

"Huh, the librarian had no idea he'd even come in. She only noticed him when locking up for the night. She panicked when he wouldn't stir."

"What have the doctors said about how exhausted he is? Have they seen this before?"

"They just said he'll need to rest at the hospital and that they've placed him on a vitamin drip. His levels are slowly coming back to normal, and they said hopefully, in the next day or two, he'll start to come around and tell us what he has done to become so tired."

"Perhaps it's just been all the stress of late? You know, all this threatening to go to the press. Maybe he just wound himself up so much his body decided it needed a rest. The mind is a peculiar thing, maybe this exhaustion thing is connected to the arguing with Polly and me."

"It's true he has been making more of an effort at home: cooking meals, doing a little housework, and then doing me. Sorry if that's a little too much information, but it's true. We've had more sexy times in the last few days than we have in the last few years. He also joined a gym, so it is possible that along with his paranoia about supernatural creatures and falling out with his daughters, plus my threat of divorce, that everything just overloaded him."

"Well, he's in the best place. Hopefully, he will continue to improve. I'll try to get over to visit him tonight."

"There's really not much point at the moment, Shelley. Not while he's unable to speak and sleeping all the time. I'll let you know when he comes round, and we can arrange for you to visit then. I know you have a lot on your plate at the moment what with arranging the wedding reception, running your business, and keeping an eye out for potential war, but thank you for offering."

We said our goodbyes and ended the call. It was proving to be a really weird morning. I decided that before I did anything else today, I would pop down to Jax's and grab a coffee and a chocolate doughnut, because I needed some normality to my day. I grabbed my purse and left my office, knocking on Lucy's door to see if she wanted anything.

My co-worker had been unusually quiet this morning. She yelled, "Come in," so I opened the door and entered her office. She was banging at her keyboard with such ferocity that I was surprised it was still intact.

"Is everything okay with you, Lucy?" I kept to the

back of the office, so I wasn't in danger of being hit by a keyboard missile if she managed to smash through it.

"Fine," she said, in that way women do which means things are most definitely not fine.

"Clearly, things are not fine. So what's going on?" I asked her. "And get on with telling me because I've already had a bitch of a Monday morning and if I don't get a coffee soon, I'm likely to blow, and right now you're the one in my firing line."

Lucy stood up from her desk, narrowing her eyes at me. "If I was still a demon right now, this situation would be even more heated than it is already. You, Shelley Landry, are currently interfering with my life and I've just about had enough of it."

"What are you talking about, Lucy?" I placed a hand on each hip. Lucy did the same. All we needed were cowboy hats and pistols and we were ready to duel.

"You decide you're throwing me a wedding reception. Then you decide it's time for Charlie to learn all about supernatural history. Therefore giving my husband an excuse to take himself away from all the wedding preparation."

I sneered at her. "What preparation? We are doing everything for you. The only thing you have to do is decide what you are wearing and Ebony is helping you with that. Then you just have to choose which Tom Hardy DVDs you want. It's hardly taxing is it? Talk about ungrateful."

"And that shows just how out of the loop you currently are. Ebony is hardly making it into the store because she's too busy shagging her husband. Instead, Alyssa is there and her choice of outfit for me is a leopard print micro dress. Every time I try to talk to Samara to ask how she is decorating the coffee shop, she just whinges on about this other Cupid rep called Rebecca and bores me to death about fucking sausage rolls when I'm not involved with the buffet. I have Jax asking me of the dietary requirements of all the different species invited, which is something Frankie could do easily, but every time I go to ask him, he's too busy finding out information or teaching your daughter. I didn't ask for this goddam reception, and I'm finding it all a large ball ache just to end up with fourteen tin openers and thirty-two tea towels as wedding presents from all the tightwad attendees who won't spend a tenner on a DVD."

"Well, I am terribly sorry that I tried to do something nice for you. I'm currently trying to protect Withernsea from war and my husband from killing my daughter's boyfriend, but let me put all this to one side to make sure you have a wedding reception to remember." I said all this with hearty sarcasm, but all Lucy said was 'Thank you' and then she sat back down. Unbelievable. She really was one on her own.

"I would like a latte please." She went back to her work.

It took every ounce of my patience to not slam the door off its hinges on my way out. The quicker I got down to the coffee shop and got my drink the better. On entering the shop, I was pleased to see that there wasn't a queue and I quickly ordered two espressos and a large Americano. I decided to sit in the coffee shop to drink them, and order Lucy's latte and take it to her when I had had a chance to calm down. Looking around, I found Maisie sitting in a corner of the coffee shop nursing a large glass of milk. I wandered over to her. She didn't usually frequent this place, so I wondered why she was hanging around here this morning. I'd probably regret asking, but something made me go over to her anyway.

"Hey, Maisie. Is it okay if I sit with you?"

Maisie looked up at me. "Sure, it would be nice to have some company."

I took the seat opposite her and looked at her closely. She definitely didn't have her usual joie de vivre. It looked like everyone was having a difficult Monday morning.

"I hope you don't mind me saying, Maisie, but you're not looking your usual self today."

She sighed. "No, I'm feeling really fed up."

"Do you mean you're feline really fed up?" I sniggered.

She gave me a look of disdain. One that only our feline friends were capable of. The look that said you are lucky to be in my company so don't push it.

"Sorry, I couldn't help myself there. What's going on?"

Maisie stretched out her limbs in an exaggerated movement. "Since Lucy and Frankie got together, I've been living next door where I have to stay a cat all the time. They are a really hot couple. I was hoping that somehow one day I'd be able to expose the truth about myself, and then hopefully expose myself, if you get me, so I could get it on with the Jason Momoa looka-like and his sexy wife. But yesterday she told him she was pregnant. So that is that. Not only does that rule them out as my sexual partners, but I heard her say that she wanted me gone, that she was going to go to Frankie and tell him he needed to make sure his cat stayed in its own home. Once again, I find myself unwanted. I wouldn't mind but I'm a damn fine pussy." I'd wondered why Maisie's glass of milk had been served on a saucer, until she picked it up, poured a little onto the saucer, and proceeded to pick up the plate and lap the milk from it. I'd never been attracted to a woman, but watching her tongue flick across the saucer, I felt the neighbour's sexy wife didn't know what she had been missing out on. Maisie placed down the saucer and sighed.

"Funnily enough, I was thinking of you the other day. I'm not sure about your present accommodation worries, but I think I might have a perfect match for you date wise. Have you been in the Indian restaurant? Because I think Rav could be your ideal date."

"Hmm. I've seen him around the place. He is quite attractive. However, spicy foods tend to upset my feline constitution. Maybe, you could introduce us? What is his house like? Is there a spare room, no dogs, a nice fire with a rug in front of it?"

"He currently lives with his mum, and I hear is desperate to get his own place. I've been told he has given up on trying to find his ideal woman. He used to be on the books of the dating agency but ceased his membership because his mother scared away every single date he had. Apparently, she wishes to choose his wife." I looked at Maisie and raised a brow. "I thought you'd be a match for an interfering mother any day of the week. But just to warn you that Rav is half-demon, proving that his mum is no walkover."

"Where might we find this Rav this morning? I think I should like to meet with him as soon as possible to see if he might be a potential partner or pet owner."

"He's usually found in the restaurant most of the time when he's not doing his duties in Hell. Theo says he spends all his spare time there in order to keep out of his mother's way."

Maisie stood up out of her seat, picked up the glass of milk and swallowed it down greedily. "What are we waiting for, Shelley? Let's go."

I figured why the hell not? I was matchmaking even though these two people weren't actually on my books. It meant Lucy's latte would have to wait which gave me a smug sense of satisfaction. I finished my drinks, said goodbye to Jax, and we made our way to Hanif's.

I knocked on the door, opened it and went inside. Usually, Rav would hurry to meet me on the rare occasions I came to see him for something, but today he wasn't there and instead I was met by a middle-aged woman holding a duster.

"Can I help you, dear?" the woman said.

"Yes, I wondered if Rav was around this morning?"

"Oh no, sorry. He's taken a week's annual leave at

short notice. Apparently, something came up. That's why I'm here."

"Oh, okay. Well, thank you anyway." I noted Maisie's look of disappointment. "It's okay, Maisie. We'll go back to the coffee shop, and I'll give him a call from there. If he's got some spare time today, you never know, he might be able to meet you for a date." Her expression brightened again.

Unfortunately, when I did ring him from the coffee shop, a female answered his phone.

"Oh, sorry. I was trying to get hold of Rav. I must've got the wrong number."

"No, this is Rav's number. He's just rather tied up at the moment," the woman informed me. I then heard a series of groans which put me in no doubt as to what she meant by tied up, and I realised that the domestic at the restaurant hadn't known how true her words were that for Rav, this week something had come up. After ending the call, I turned around to Maisie and apologised for getting her hopes up for no reason.

"Oh no worries. Who's saying I would have liked him, anyway. Thank you for trying."

"Well, if there's anything else I can do. You can always come look at the books to see who else is free. If you join the agency, we'll be able to input your details.

You'd have prospects coming out of your ears, I'm sure."

"I'll think about it." Her stomach growled. "Meanwhile, any chance you'd buy me a piece of haddock from the chippy?"

I finally returned to the office and dropped a latte off with Lucy who didn't even look up to say thank you. Then I called Samara, Ebony, and Jax and told them that they'd better make sure they'd done what they'd promised for the wedding reception and not to expect too much in the way of gratitude from the newlywed.

I stayed behind a little to get caught up on work. The truth was I didn't feel like going home if I was about to witness World War Three. Finally, when I could put it off no longer, I whizzed back to the farmhouse.

I found my husband admiring the craftsmanship of Charlie's chair. The piece was spectacular. So much so, that I only received a cursory hello from Theo before he went back to looking at it.

"Thank goodness that this does still look beautiful out of the sea," he said. "I do believe I am going to commission your boyfriend to make a chair for each room here on the bed and breakfast side. Could you bring him here, or take me to him so I can discuss this? I may even get him to do headboards for each room. Oh the possibilities."

Charlie looked at me from over her father's head, shrugging her shoulders.

"You'll see him at the wedding reception on Friday, won't you? You can talk to him then," she told him.

"Oh, yes. Of course. Perfect. That gives me time to go around the house and make a list of what I might like him to make. Splendid. Thank you, Charlie. I'm excited. Seems you have a good one there after all." He patted her on the shoulder. "Right, I'm just off to my office for an hour." With that, he left the room, kissing my cheek on his way past.

"What the hell just happened? He's been possessed. Where's your real father?" I asked Charlie. "We said to look out for unusual behaviour and there it is."

"Mum, he said he understood that I had grown up and realised he was being stupid, and that he didn't like it, but as long as I was happy and Kai treated me okay, he would try to make peace with it. Then he stared at the chair for an hour."

"Thank goodness for that, because there's enough to do without fearing your father is going to lynch your boyfriend." I proceeded to tell her about Mark being in hospital.

"Oh, that's awful. I can't say I'm keen on him, but Debbie seems okay these days. It must be a worry."

"Well, apparently, he's joined a gym to try to tone up, among other things. Sounds like he's overdone it. Anyway, I don't know about you, but my arse wants to sit itself on the sofa and watch television."

"I'm going back to Kai's."

I smiled. "You might have been as well leaving that chair where it was."

She grinned back. "He's making me another for at the cottage."

Stepping forward, I wrapped her in my arms. "Go on. You get going and enjoy yourself. I'll call you if you're needed for any Withernsea woes. If I don't see you before, I'll catch you Friday at the reception. Eight pm at Jax's.

"Wouldn't miss it for the world. It'll be nice for us all to get together for something good."

If only that had proved to be the case...

CHAPTER 18

SHELLEY

In the end, my *Female Entrepreneurs do it with their Colleagues* girlies had knocked it out of the park. Samara had decorated the cafe in soft pinks and whites. There was heart-shaped bunting, pretty white lace vintage tablecloths, heart-shaped confetti, and soft mood lighting. Jax set the buffet out against the back wall. The food was laid out in sections catering for all species. When the bride and groom arrived, Frankie was dressed in a sharp, navy-blue suit; and Lucy was wearing the most gorgeous white satin dress. It had thin straps, a glittering bodice, and the bottom of the dress was covered in white feathers. On her head was a small tiara, and her bobbed, ginger hair had been styled in ringlets by Charlie. Most of us had arrived before the newlyweds and so on entry we all burst into a round of applause and cheers. Tristan had taken charge of the music and Bruno Mars' *Marry You* played out across the cafe. It was very unnerving to see Lucy beaming, but right now the most massive smile shone on her face as she clasped Frankie's hand and walked around greeting their guests.

I'd been sure to reserve a space for Kim, and she was currently sitting on the cafe sofa. Darius' mother was looking after the triplets for the evening and Kim had given me a full-blown account on how hard it was to express milk for all three of them and get it bottled up for her mother-in-law, and that she hoped we all realised what she sacrificed in order for Lucy to have a good time. At that point I'd made my excuses and had gone to check if Jax needed any help.

I needed to make my own contribution now. While the newlyweds were in the cafe, I needed to whizz to their house and get their bedroom prepared for the honeymoon night. I let Theo know where I was going and then I whizzed through to their house.

I appeared in the hallway and the first thing I noted was the sound of a cat screaming. Maisie! Shit! It sounded like Maisie was in trouble. I ran upstairs and headed in the direction of the spare room where the wails were coming from. Kicking open the door, with my magic at my fingertips, I found a tabby cat mounting a black one.

"Oh my fucking god. I am so sorry." I backed out of the room quickly. On the landing, I took a deep breath, and made my way to Frankie and Lucy's bedroom. I sprinkled rose petals across their bed and hung a 'Just Married' banner on the wall above the headboard. From my bag, I took out two engraved champagne glasses–one that said 'Mrs Love' and one that said 'Mr Love' and placed them at the right-hand side of the bed on the bedside table, along with a bottle of champagne. At the left-hand side of the bed, I placed a box of chocolates.

The bedroom door opened, and Maisie walked in. She didn't have on a stitch of clothing, and her black hair was mussed up.

"Oh, so that's why you're here. Shoot, I totally forgot, it's the wedding reception, isn't it? I'd better get dressed for it."

"Well, just for you to get dressed at all would be a bonus right now."

"God, some of you are just so prudish. You know this is how you were born right? This is your natural state. But I'll put some clothes on. Could I catch a lift with you back to the reception? It'll be a lot quicker if you do that whizzing thing."

When she did get dressed, Maisie returned dressed in a tight black lace dress that left little to the imagination. I was about to tell her to change into something else when my phone rang. I looked down at the caller display to see the name Debbie flashing. For a split second I thought about ignoring the call because there was enough happening right now, but concern that Mark could have taken a turn for the worse made me feel guilty, so I answered.

"Hey. Is everything okay?"

"Oh, Shelley. Things are not good at all. I honestly do not know what to do. Your father has begun to speak, but it's all nonsense. He's telling them he's been possessed by the devil and that it was the devil who left him there in the library. All this supernatural stuff and the worry has obviously got to his brain. They've called in psychiatrists. It's so upsetting, Shelley, I just want to cry. He's clutching my arm, eyes wide and fearful, begging me to believe him."

This was all I needed right now. "Well, hopefully, the psychiatrist will be able to get him on some medication and soon you'll have your old husband back."

"Well, I hope it's not my old husband. I hope when he recovers, he's back to being the one he's been this week. Anyway, he's demanding to see you, saying that you can help him. He believes you can cleanse his body of the evil."

"I'll come and see him in the morning. Right now, I'm in the middle of the wedding celebration for Frankie and Lucy. I suggest you try your best to get a good night's sleep and we'll see what tomorrow brings."

"Thank you so much, Shelley. I'm still at the hospital. But at least now I can tell him he'll see you in the morning and that might settle him for the night."

Ending the call, I sighed.

"What was all that about?" Maisie asked.

"Nothing that can't wait," I told her, "Come on, let's get back to the party."

The party was in full swing by the time we returned. I'd just let Theo know I was back, when a middle-aged guy walked towards me. His hair was short and pale blonde, and he was on the plump side with cherubic rosy cheeks. It crossed my mind that maybe his cholesterol might need checking sometime soon.

"Shelley Landry?" he queried, holding out his hand.

"Yes, that would be me, and you are?"

But as I took his hand in mine, I became completely full of the warm fuzzies and love for everyone, so I knew who he was before he said it.

"I'm Cupid."

"Oh my goodness. What an honour. I am so very pleased to meet you." I actually curtsied to the guy.

"No need to do that, my dear. I wanted to come to see you about the recent hiccup with a couple of my employees. I got wind of the wedding reception, and couldn't resist calling in. Lovely buffet. I have congratulated Jax on it. Simply delightful."

"Oh, okay." I tried to form more words, but my mouth just opened and closed without managing to produce anything of worth.

"Love a good buffet. I quite often crash engagement and wedding celebrations. Perk of the job."

That certainly explained his appearance. Hopefully, his kind of supernatural didn't have to worry about potential heart attacks from eating too many fatty foods and sweet treats.

"Erm, are you wanting me to close my dating agency?" I asked him. "Is it interfering in the world of Cupid?"

He laughed heartily. "Oh goodness me, Shelley. No, not at all. You're helping bring love. No way do I want you to stop. No, if anything this spat with

Samara and Rebecca has done Cupid Inc a huge favour."

"It has?" I couldn't be any more confused right now.

"Yes. Rebecca came to see me. It appears she'd had a lovely little chat with your daughter. Little smasher you've got there and she and that boy with her are destined to love strong. I can feel it. Anyhow, back to the chat. Rebecca has suggested that my cupid team begin to specialise in the people you can't get dates for. So anyone who for whatever reason is struggling to be matched up, just let Rebecca know and she'll get on it."

My brow creased. "Rebecca? Not Samara?"

Cupid's face went stern. "Samara has not been doing her work properly for a while now. She is being sent to training school in London, and then will be placed on probation for a time. There are no dating agencies in the area, and she will be set a series of challenges. I have to show the rest of the Cupid reps that they can't get away with being lazy and acting stupid about it."

I'd thought it was strange that Samara had dressed the place up and then left. She'd yet to join the party. She must be well pissed off at having to leave her home. She loved Withernsea.

"However long she is gone for depends on her. Rebecca is only covering the area temporarily along with Hornsea. Hopefully, Samara will learn her lesson and return to deal with your truly undateables."

He looked at his watch. "Right, I must dash. Lots of celebrations on a weekend that need my attention. Until we meet again, thank you, Shelley, for bringing love to the world." He touched my arm. "Hopefully, I can bring some extra love to yours." A feeling of warmth zipped through my body and once again I felt the love for my family and friends amplified. With a wink he walked out of the door.

Walking over to my husband, I took his hand in mine. "Want to get out of here soon, Theo?"

"I'd love to, but I think we might be missed. We need to stay until the end."

Theo never wanted to stay at a party. I realised he was watching Charlie and Kai. "Let them just get on with their lives." I held his arm.

He placed his hand over mine. "Oh, I just haven't had a chance to talk to Kai about the furniture yet. I hope to do so before I leave. Only the sooner he gets the order done the better. It's not going to be long now before I open our B&B, Shelley. I've been designing and ordering the brochures today."

"Theo, that's fantastic. Okay, I'll get Charlie. I

don't think she's had anything to eat yet, and you can chat with Kai."

"Thank you. That would be most helpful."

Charlie looked over at the buffet. "Mum, is Jax trying to tempt fate, because that looks like a large plate of sausage rolls to me?"

I laughed. "She's become addicted to the ones Rebecca sent Samara. She was annoyed that she couldn't eat one of them in case they had been poisoned, so she took the card and ordered some herself. I think she's going to add them to the cafe's menu. I presume Ebony's sausage roll predictions are over and done with now, and we can once again enjoy a good roll." My daughter sniggered. Then she looked around the room.

"Mom, why is Dad directing Kai out of the doorway?"

My jaw dropped. "Oh shit. Your dad is bloody clever, I'll give him that. I completely fell for the 'I want him to make the B&B furniture' malarkey. I've been hoodwinked." Legging it over to the doorway and out into the street, I saw Theo had poor Kai held up by his shirt collar.

"You have claimed my daughter's innocence and now you shall marry her," Theo hissed, his eyes blazing red.

"Dad, oh my god, Dad. Put him down," Charlie screamed. When Theo didn't take any notice, she thrust out her blue webs and peeled him off her boyfriend. It was the first time I had seen her in control of her powers, and I realised that the work she'd done over the last few days had paid off. Theo looked shocked as he stood there wrapped up in his daughter's handiwork.

"Could you let me go, Charlie, please? I'm only doing this for your honour."

"Theo," I yelled. "You were not a virgin when we married, and neither was I." Yet again, I felt I should put my fist in my mouth to stop myself from digging a deeper hole. Oh God, even my thoughts were inappropriate. I hoped he hadn't heard them as my guard was down. A hiss told me he had, so I immediately blocked my thoughts off.

"Dad." Charlie then did the weirdest but most amazing thing. She sent out an icy wisp that travelled down her father's body and cooled his temper. His eyes went back to their normal brown and his fangs retracted. "What you have just done to Kai is inexcusable. He has been nothing but a gentleman from day one, and I seduced him. You understand that? I'll say it again. I. Seduced. Him." She kept him wrapped in tendrils of the cool wisps. "Last night, Kai proposed to me, and I accepted. TAKE THAT SMUG GRIN OFF YOUR FACE, DAD. I've a good mind to unaccept it now, but I can't because I love him too much. Now please can we go back inside and enjoy the party?"

"Now you want to enjoy the party?" We turned to find Lucy and half the guests outside. "You announce your engagement at my wedding do. Talk about a topper. Not content with being queen and taking my husband's attention from me, you want to take the attention away again tonight too. Disgraceful." Lucy stomped off back inside.

A terrifying, chilling scream came from indoors and we all ran in to find Ebony on her knees, looking in severe pain while clutching her head. "The heat. The heat. I feel like I'm burning from the inside out." Her eyes went wide and then rolled up in her head and she passed out. The new Satan walked through the door.

"Oh dear. My apologies. I've not quite got the hang of controlling my heat levels on earth yet," he said. "Sorry to intrude, but I wondered if I might have a word with you, Shelley?" He spotted the buffet. "Oh my, it's years since I've had a good British buffet. Do you mind?" He looked around.

"Help yourself," Jax told him.

We walked over to the table, and I watched as we both dived for a sausage roll at the same time. Our hands collided and I recoiled at his touch, getting a reading of who was really in the body of the new Satan.

The old one.

His expression told me he knew I knew.

"It was nice knowing you. Actually, that's a lie, you've been a pain in the arse from start to finish. See ya, wouldn't want to be ya," he said, and he sent a shot of flames out in my direction.

The pain was so bad. My last thoughts were that I'd forgotten I was no longer the powerful wyvern I used to be. Now I was only a witch/vampire hybrid. Everything went black...

And then everything went white, and I was standing in a completely white room at the side of Angel Sophia.

"Oh no. Am I dead?" I asked her.

"Shelley, you're already dead. You're a vampire."

"Oh yeah. Well did I succumb to his flames though?"

"No. He needs to stake you through the heart. Always has been overconfident that one."

"So where am I?"

"You're in a holding bay here in Heaven. You were wrapped in hellfire which is agonising, and I was asked to bring you up here to keep you comfortable until it leaves your system. We only found out fifteen minutes ago that he was back. That he had taken over the body of the current Satan."

"How did you find out?"

"Hell has changed drastically in the last few days. It had been running more as a democracy and then all of a sudden, we're back to having a tyrannical, egotistical leader. It wasn't rocket science to work it out. What I don't know is how he's managed it."

"I broke my agreement with him. I matchmade my sister with Drake. A human and a supernatural."

"Still, there must have been a glitch in the system because once vanquished, he should have stayed that way. Not been able to be brought back. The elders are looking into it. However." She picked up a scroll from the seat beside her and passed it to me. "While you are here, read this. We have had student scholars reading the ancient files and transcribing them onto more modern systems. This is from our archives."

After unrolling the scroll, I read it.

To one there will be a blessing. And from this shall come forth a child of the angels. This child shall hold immense

supernatural power, and at the time of the Great War,
will inherit her celestial inheritance.

The balance shall be restored.

I stared at Sophia.

"Charlie?"

She nodded.

"Charlie."

CHAPTER 19

CHARLIE

It all happened so fast. One minute I'd been dealing with my father. Then the next, Ebony was passed out on the floor, and the devil walked in and shot fire at my mum. She fell to the floor, smoke pouring from her eyes, ears, mouth, and nostrils.

"Muuuuuuuummmm," I screamed.

Satan spun around.

"Charlie, babes. We've not met. I'm Satan. Not the one whose body I currently inhabit, although I have to say it's not bad. Not bad at all. But the one who had a bit of beef with your mother. Think that beef is well cooked now, don't you?"

My father ran to my mother's side.

"Oh look, how sweet. Little Theo running to his

newly barbecued wife's side. Probably too late, Theo, mate. I can do a two-for-one deal if you like?" Flames threatened at his fingertips.

That was it. The coffee shop erupted and every single person in the room began to surge towards Satan. Using my wyvern powers, I froze them all in place, looking at them in mid-step: my family and friends. Every single one of them, with the exception of Ebony and my mother, were prepared to battle on my behalf. I felt the power surge through my veins as I embraced all of their battle cries and powers. Every single species, supe and human alike was joining the battle and their power sang in my veins. I waited to turn into my wyvern, but instead a brilliant white light sank into me, and white feathers fell as if from the sky, falling to the coffee shop floor like a carpet of snow.

Satan's eyes widened. "Nice party trick." He shot out flames at me.

I caught them, turning them to ice with the power of the sea. Then the sirens call came through me as I sang a melody that brought Satan to his knees, his hands over his ears. "Stop. Stop it."

A clawed fist, a gift from the shifters appeared, and I walked over to Satan and swiped across his abdomen. He screamed a gutteral unearthly scream as a slash appeared in his skin. It filled with the bright, white light.

Words appeared in my mind, a spell, my witchcraft heritage. I began to speak them:

> *"Oh son of darkness*
> *Creator of destruction*
> *Now it is time to heed my instruction*
> *Every atom*
> *Every cell*
> *Come to me as I weave my spell."*

Satan's mouth opened and with a silent scream he began to disintegrate from the inside out. I continued.

> *"Each single particle*
> *Travel far and wide*
> *Never again to assemble side by side*
> *One in each kingdom*
> *One in each realm*
> *Locked within the bark of an enchanted elm."*

The red cells he had broken into danced before me and turned white and then they shot through the walls. One small cell remained and although it should not have been visible to my eye, it was suspended in the air and magnified so I could see it.

> *"The last of you*
> *The evil one*
> *Shall stay in heaven until time is done*
> *You will never escape*
> *Your time here is ended*
> *Now balance will restore*
> *As Fate intended."*

With that the feathers swirled up from the ground, wrapping around the final cell and they disappeared through the ceiling. He was gone. It was done.

The freeze on the room lifted as people surged forward before realising that he was no longer there. Then they looked at me and dropped to their knees.

As I looked down at myself, I saw that I was glowing with a white light from the inside out. I heard the words 'My Queen' fall from everyone's lips.

Then the white light slowly dimmed until it was no more, and Ebony and my mum came around with large intakes of air.

My father took my mum straight to the caves. Frankie, who used to be a physician, checked over Ebony to make sure she was okay. My grandparents, Dylan and Margret, came rushing towards me, Kai not far behind.

"Charlie. Are you okay? My goodness. It was so strange. We came to help you and then it was like we froze. I could see and hear what was happening, but I couldn't move a muscle," my grandma said.

"Granddaughter, you were simply amazing. You must conserve your powers for the next couple of days; let Kai look after you. Come, we will drop you off at the farmhouse as I'm sure your parents will wish to see you as soon as your mum is discharged from the caves."

The door opening made us all jump. Samara stomped through, a fawn-coloured Whippet at her heels. The dog immediately ran up to Maisie and barked its head off.

"For fuck's sake, every time we see a cat it's the same. Johnny, you are driving me insane. I'll have to put you in a kennel if you can't behave."

"You could try putting it on that lead you've got in your hand. That might be a start in getting him to behave," I told her. "Anyway, why have you called your dog the same name as your husband? That's got to be confusing."

"That's because it is my husband," Samara yelled. "It's part of my stupid punishment for not being a good Cupid. Apparently, the managers don't believe I should have a happy love life when I'm not working hard enough to make sure anyone else is. Therefore, they have turned Johnny into a Whippet and he won't turn back into my husband until I have done their stupid training. Now, what does a girl have to do to get a drink around here because I've had a really difficult day."

I couldn't help it. I burst into laughter, and within a minute the whole cafe was laughing along with me.

The End.

Can Samara get her husband back and learn to love Cupiding again? What secret is Shelley hiding? Find out in book seven of the Supernatural Dating Agency series:

Acting Cupid.
(The Cupid Inc duet has been completely reworked to form part of the Supernatural Dating Agency series)

For a glimpse of life before the vampire got his wife, join my mailing list and receive the short story prequel *Dating Sucks*:

geni.us/andiemlongparanormal

About Andie

Andie M. Long lives in Sheffield, UK, with her long-suffering partner, her son, and a gorgeous Whippet furbaby. She's addicted to coffee and Toblerone.

When not being partner, mother, or writer, she can usually be found wasting far too much time watching TikTok.

Andie's Reader Group on Facebook
www.facebook.com/groups/haloandhornshangout

TikTok and Instagram
@andieandangelbooks

Paranormal Romance
BY ANDIE M. LONG

Supernatural Dating Agency

The Vampire wants a Wife

A Devil of a Date

Hate, Date, or Mate

Here for the Seer

Didn't Sea it Coming

Phwoar and Peace

Also on audio, paperback, and a complete series ebook
bundle available.

The Paranormals

Hex Factor

Heavy Souls

We Wolf Rock You

Satyrday Night Fever

Also in paperback. Complete series ebook available.

Sucking Dead

Suck My Life – available on audio.

My Vampire Boyfriend Sucks

Sucking Hell

Suck it Up

Hot as Suck

Filthy Rich Vampires – Reverse Harem

Royal Rebellion (Last Rites/First Rules duet) – Time Travel Young Adult Fantasy

Immortal Bite – Gothic romance

Printed in Great Britain
by Amazon